THE BOOK OF MORMON SLEUTH

BOOKS BY C.B. ANDERSEN

THE BOOK OF MORMON SLEUTH

The Forgotten Treasure

C. B. ANDERSEN

DESERET
BOOK

SALT LAKE CITY, UTAH

*For my forebears, near and far, whose choices
have brought the gospel of Jesus Christ into my life*

Library of Congress Cataloging-in-Publication Data

Andersen, C. B. (Carl Blaine), 1961-
 The forgotten treasure / C. B. Andersen.
  p. cm. — (The Book of Mormon sleuth ; 4)
 On a vacation to visit Mormon historical sites in New York and Ohio, the Andrews family endures stalking by a bushy-bearded man and an unexpected swim at Niagara Falls while tracking down a treasure held by a long-lost relative.
 ISBN 1-59038-314-1 (pbk.)
 [1. Mormons—Fiction. 2. Family life—Fiction. 3. Vacations—Fiction.] I. Title.
 PZ7.A51887Fo 2004
 [Fic]—dc22
                            2004000908

Printed in the United States of America   54459
Malloy Lithographing Incorporated, Ann Arbor, MI

10   9   8   7   6   5   4   3   2   1

Contents

Acknowledgments

I gratefully acknowledge the outstanding efforts of the publishing and marketing department staffs at Deseret Book, especially Emily Watts for her creative vision, Richard Peterson for his editorial expertise, Tonya Facemyer for her typesetting skills, Richard Erickson for the sensational cover designs that have attracted countless readers, and both Kathie Terry and Laurel Christensen for their commitment to getting these books into the hands of as many readers as possible. These are people of the highest caliber whom I am pleased to call friends.

CHAPTER 1

The Kidnapped Caller

A couple of years ago, Mom bought a huge, black, unabridged dictionary for Dad for Christmas. I think that's the most excited I've ever seen him get about any gift he has ever received. Go figure. Dad *adores* that dictionary, pulling it out often and at the strangest times. For example, when he's talking about something and one of the younger kids asks what one of his words means, he will do his best to define the word and then look it up in the dictionary and read all the definitions out loud to us. It seems to me that if he has to look the word up to explain it, then he probably had no business using the word in the first place. One word I wish he would look up, though, is the word *vacation*.

According to that huge, black, unabridged dictionary (that belongs on the bookshelf in our family room, but is rarely found there) the word *vacation* means "freedom from any activity" or "a period of rest"—it is a "time of relaxation or recreation." If that is true, then *not one* of the last three family "vacations" we've had would qualify as a vacation. There was absolutely nothing relaxing about any of them, and there was precious little recreation going on, either.

This year, though, it looked like Dad had things arranged so that at least *he* would be able to relax for a while, even if no one else really could. And, to be honest, Dad had been *way* uptight and needed serious relaxation time. It all started the day Mom took me to the driver's license office, then announced at dinnertime, "Jeff got his learner's permit today."

My whole life I had known Dad was uptight, but I had never seen the look of panic that came into his eyes as he heard those words. The color immediately drained from his face, and he struggled to swallow the food in his mouth, which had apparently suddenly doubled in size and gotten very dry. As soon as he could speak, Dad quietly asked, "*Jeff* did? D-did they lower the age?"

"No," Mom smiled. "He'll be sixteen in three months."

Dad quickly touched his left thumb to three fingers on the same hand, looked over at me, and said weakly, "That's great, Jeff." This was followed by a loud gulp. "I guess it's time to start practicing together." I don't think he ate anything the rest of the meal. And it's too bad, too, because he probably could have used the energy later that evening when we went driving together, and he kept trying to push his foot through the floor on the passenger side. He did it every time he apparently thought I ought to be going a lot slower or stopping a lot sooner. All that pushing must have given him a pretty good workout because his face was all sweaty by the time we finished.

I'd like to be able to say that things got better the more we practiced, but they didn't. And after I had actually *passed* the driving test and gotten my real license, then he seemed even more stressed out by the thought that I could now legally drive places without him being there to operate his imaginary brake pedal.

So when Dad announced to us the plan for our vacation this year, he acted quite pleased with himself. The entire family would be flying round-trip to Cleveland, Ohio, using frequent-flyer miles that he had accumulated over several years of business trips. In Cleveland we were going to rent a van and drive to Church history sites between Kirtland, Ohio, and Palmyra, New York. We were also going to visit some other places, such as Niagara Falls.

"We're renting a twelve-passenger van exactly like ours," Dad smiled, "so everything will be just like what we're used to."

I wasn't sure if that was a good thing or not, even though Dad acted like *he* thought it was.

"Will I get to drive the rental van sometimes?" I asked. "Since it's just like ours?"

With a deep and contented sigh, Dad answered, "No, Jeff. The rental company won't even rent to anyone under the age of twenty-five, so only Mom and I will be driving." With another deep, happy sigh, he added, "Sorry about that!"

He really didn't seem all that sorry about it, but the relaxed look on his face reminded me of how much lower his stress level had been before I got my learner's permit, so I was happy he was going to get a break. Besides, we were only going to be gone for a couple of weeks.

"If we were taking our own van," Mom added, "we would certainly let you drive part of the time."

Dad shot a glance in her direction that gave me the impression he didn't agree with her comment. My brother Brandon, who is just a year younger than I am, said, "I'm glad we've finally given up on trying to go to Alaska."

Both of the previous two summers we had attempted to collect on a free Alaskan cruise that Dad had won, but the experience taught me that—just like the saying goes—there's no such thing as a free lunch. In our case, we could never get the free dinners or breakfasts, either. Or anything else that was supposedly included on this free cruise that we won.

"That's right," Dad said to Brandon. "Mom and I have agreed that it's time to attempt a *relaxed* vacation that includes very little chance of danger."

Those were "famous last words" if I'd ever heard them. It seems like whenever Dad makes a comment like that, he is not just setting us up for disaster. He's *inviting* it!

3

"Sort of like when we went to Nauvoo three years ago?" I asked. "That attempt pretty much failed, though, didn't it?"

When I was thirteen—the year before we made our first Alaska attempt—our family vacation was visiting our Great-aunt Ella's dairy farm in Iowa. She was quite old at the time and decided to give something very valuable to Brandon: a 170-year-old copy of the first printing of the Book of Mormon. It was great at first, but then along came this lunatic historian-guy who was after some old paper that was with the book. He thought that it would lead him to some "secret treasure." Well, it didn't. What it did do was just about get me and Brandon killed. After it was all over, and that weirdo, Dr. Anthony, had been taken care of, Dad convinced Brandon that he ought to donate the document to the Church. I don't think that any of us had really thought much more about it until two guys from the FBI showed up at our door one evening. It was just a few days before we were to leave on this "relaxed vacation that includes very little chance of danger."

Shauna, my sister, who had just finished her first year at BYU, was sitting at the kitchen table showing Brandon and me this cool laptop computer that she had borrowed from another BYU student. He let her borrow it for our vacation so that we could watch DVDs on the plane and in the van. Shauna is a computer science major, and this guy is a graduate student and also a teacher's aide for a couple of her classes.

"Look at this cool program he's working on," Shauna said. "He has a government grant to work on voice-matching software."

"What's that?" Brandon asked.

"It's a system for analyzing recorded voices," Shauna explained, "and then matching them with voices that have already been stored in a database. It can be used to identify people by their voice, when you're not sure who they are. Each person's voice is unique, kind of like fingerprints."

"Cool!" Brandon said.

"He showed me how to work it," Shauna said. She frowned just a little and added, "I think he was trying to impress me."

"Looks like it worked," I said.

Shauna smirked.

"I still can't believe he let you borrow it," I said.

Shauna frowned again and said, "He told me it would give him an excuse to come see me when we get back."

Brandon and I exchanged glances, but didn't bother to state the obvious.

"Here," she said as she made a couple of clicks on the computer. "Now it's recording what I'm saying. When it's done, it will try to match my voice to what is already in its database."

She clicked a couple of more times and said, "Now it's trying to match my voice."

Brandon and I just stared at the screen. Within a couple of seconds, a message popped up that read, "Voice match probability: seventy-two percent—Shauna the Beautiful."

"Ha!" I laughed. "He calls you *Shauna the Beautiful?*"

"Oh, yeah," Shauna mumbled, "I forgot about that." Then, louder, she added, "But that's not the point."

"He's *in love* with you!" Brandon guffawed.

Shauna shook her head in frustration. "No," she grunted. "He's just—that way with me. It doesn't mean anything."

"Maybe not to *you*," I said, "but I'll bet it means something to *him.*"

She looked slightly nauseated as she tried to explain, "It's just because there aren't very many girls majoring in computer science. It doesn't matter." Heaving a heavy sigh, she pointed to the screen and said, "Look at this. It knows who I am!"

"I think it only knows who seventy-two percent of you is," I said.

Brandon laughed. Shauna shook her head again and said, "It's just because the sample of my voice wasn't very long. The more data it has, the better chance the program has to make a more certain match."

"That is so cool!" said Brandon. "How does it work?"

"That's the best part," Shauna explained. "He uses what he calls the *timbre*. It's like the difference between the sound of a note played on a piano and the same note played on something else—like a cello or a violin. He's developed a way to describe those differences mathematically, and that's what he has stored in the database."

"Will it work on us, too?" Brandon asked, "or is it only designed for people whose last name is 'the Beautiful'?"

"Funny, Bran," Shauna said.

"It's probably only designed for Shauna!" I blurted out.

"No," she said with disgust. "I'll show you."

Shauna was in the middle of recording both Brandon and me when Mom and Dad came into the kitchen with two men that we had never seen before. They were both wearing dark suits and carrying briefcases. I didn't know how long they had been there because I hadn't even heard the doorbell ring.

"Kids, these men are FBI agents," Dad said. "This is Agent Jones and this is Agent Sniff." At least I think he said *Sniff*—I guess he might have said *Smith*. But since the man gave a huge sniff at the same time Dad said his name, I was never quite sure what his name was. Maybe I just thought I heard *Sniff* because that's when he sniffed.

Agent Jones smiled, but the other agent was as stiff as a board. (Maybe Dad had said Agent *Stiff*.) Even though the two agents were dressed basically the same, they looked very different from each other. Agent Jones looked quite a bit older and seemed much more friendly. His suit looked like he had owned it for quite a few years—decades maybe. He was clean and neat, but his shirt looked well-worn, and his tie seemed to me like it was already out of style.

His shoes looked like the soles had been replaced one too many times.

Agent Stiff, though, looked like he just finished a photo shoot for a fashion magazine cover. All four buttons on the front of his suit jacket were done up. His shirt was crisp, looking like it had just been starched and ironed. His tie looked brand-new and very expensive. And on the top of both of his shoes were two little leather tassels. He looked around the room as though he were afraid something might accidentally brush against his clothing and he would need to rush immediately to the dry cleaner.

Mom continued, "Apparently a man from Salt Lake City is missing, and they are wondering if we know anything about it."

"Who is it?" Brandon asked. "Was he kidnapped?"

"Those are good questions, son," said the older man, Agent Jones. "His name is Paul Mauer. He's been missing for three days."

"And why would we know something about it?" I asked.

"Another good question," said Agent Photo Shoot, turning to me. "We have been attempting to contact everyone who Mr. Mauer might have been in contact with over the last week. According to phone company records, he made two calls to your home the day before he disappeared."

There was silence in the room for a moment.

"Does anyone remember speaking with a Paul Mauer four days ago?" asked Agent Jones. We all looked around at each other and shook our heads.

"Is there anyone else who lives here who might have answered the phone when he called?" Sniff asked.

"Yes," Mom said, heading toward the bedrooms, "we have three other children. I'll get them."

"Do you have an answering machine?" asked Agent Jones with a smile.

"Yes," Dad said.

7

"Oh, wait," Shauna breathed. "I think I remember saving a message from someone."

"Would it still be saved?" asked Agent Fashion Magazine, picking an imaginary piece of lint from his jacket sleeve—maybe it wasn't imaginary, but I didn't see anything.

"Oh, I'm sure of it," answered Dad, reaching for the cordless phone. "We rarely listen to our messages—new or old." He gave sort of a weak smile as he dialed the messaging service and put the phone to his ear. He began listening to messages and pushing buttons. A few moments later Mom returned with eleven-year-old Meg, nine-year-old Chelsea, and seven-year-old Danny.

"Do each of *you* answer the phone on occasion?" asked Agent Sniff stiffly.

They all stared up at him with wide eyes and open mouths.

"They do," Mom answered for them.

"Brandon," Dad said, the phone still pressed to his ear, "did Patrick get ahold of you about his missing sock?"

Brandon's mouth dropped partway open and he looked like he was trying to remember.

"Craig," Mom said to Dad, "I think that can wait until later, can't it?"

"Oh, oh, of course," Dad laughed slightly, glancing at the FBI agents. He pushed a button as he said, "I'll save that one again, Bran. You can listen to it later."

Dad listened and pushed a few more buttons before suddenly saying, "Here it is!" He squinted as he listened. I'm not sure if squinting helped his hearing or not. "Shall I put it on speakerphone?" he asked.

"Please," smiled Agent Jones.

Dad pushed another button and then placed the cordless phone down on the kitchen table.

"Hi—hello? Is this the home of the Andrews family?" came an unfamiliar voice from the phone. "My name is Paul Mauer. I work in the Church Historian's Office in Salt Lake City. I've been reviewing a document you donated to the archives a couple of years ago, and I've discovered something about Elias Franzen that you may find interesting. I'll try back again later. 'Bye."

"What time was that message received?" asked Agent Stiff with a sniff.

"I think it said about noon," Dad replied.

"So that was the first call," said the agent, looking over some papers he had pulled from his briefcase. "The next call was made about 3:30 the same day." Looking up, he asked, "Was there another message?"

Dad played with the phone for about half a minute and then said, "No, nothing else."

"Who is generally home at that time of day?" asked Agent Jones.

"All the kids are out of school by then," Mom answered.

"Does anyone remember answering a call from this man later that day?" he asked.

There was silence for a moment.

"I do," answered Meg softly. Her eyes were still wide. Both agents turned toward Meg and seemed to loom over her. She looked tiny next to these full-grown men who suddenly were *very* interested in what she had to say. She chose to look at Agent Jones.

"Do you remember what he said?" he asked.

"He said he wanted to talk to my dad or to Brandon," Meg answered shyly.

"Were they not home?" asked the agent.

"Brandon was," Meg said, "but he wouldn't come to the phone until I found out who the man was and what he wanted."

Everyone turned to look at Brandon, who suddenly got very defensive. But Meg continued before Brandon could say anything.

"I asked the man to tell me his name again," explained Meg,

9

"and to tell me what he wanted, so he just told *me* the message instead of waiting for Brandon."

Brandon looked like he was afraid he might be getting in trouble for this, but he lucked out.

"Did the man say *what* he had discovered?" asked Agent Smith.

"Words," squeaked Meg.

"Words?" He sniffed.

"Uh-huh," nodded Meg. "Words."

"I don't understand what you mean," said Agent Smith. "The document was covered with words. Is that all he said?"

Meg gulped. "He said that there were words on the side of the paper that you couldn't see unless there was a bright light shining behind the paper."

"Along the edge?" asked Agent Jones.

"Uh-huh," nodded Meg again.

"This is ridiculous," scoffed Agent Smith. "Sounds like some Boy Scout came along with his magic, invisible ink."

"No," said Meg with more confidence. "He said he didn't think it was supposed to be invisible. He said he thought it was just bad ink and that it had just gone away because it was written a long time ago."

"Do you mean it faded over time?" asked Dad.

"Yeah," nodded Meg. "I remember now. He said it was faded."

Agent Smith suddenly seemed interested again. "So what did the writing say?" he asked, leaning over her once more.

"I don't remember," Meg confessed.

The agent rolled his eyes and looked over at Agent Jones. After a big sigh, he looked at Dad and asked, "Are you sure there are no more messages?"

"Nothing," said Dad, glancing at the phone still in his hand.

Turning back to Meg, he asked again, "Are you sure you don't remember what the words were?"

Meg opened her mouth as if to say something, but then

hesitated before finally closing it again and shaking her head back and forth. "I don't remember," she said again.

Agent Stiff acted annoyed. Turning to Dad he said in a stern voice, "Let us know whatever you can get out of her." He made it sound like he expected Dad to chain her up and torture her or something.

Mom seemed a little irritated at the guy's attitude.

"All right," replied Dad.

Reaching into the outside chest pocket of his perfect suit, Agent Stiff pulled out a business card and handed it to Dad. "Call me at this number anytime night or day as soon as you have any more information." He turned and headed for the door.

As Agent Smith walked out the door, Agent Jones stooped down next to Meg. With a smile and a wink he said, "Don't worry about it, honey. We appreciate your help." He glanced toward the front door. Agent Smith had gone outside, leaving the door open, and was walking briskly toward their car. Looking up at Mom and Dad, the agent added in a quiet voice, "I really don't think it matters much. But if you come across any more information, please do give Agent Tassel-Shoes a call."

"Agent Tassel-Shoes?" asked Mom.

He stood and smiled, answering, "He doesn't know that's what we call him. But we do all sort of give him a hard time about how he dresses. He's single. I guess he can afford it." Turning to leave, he shook Dad's hand. "Thanks again for your help."

After they had driven away and Dad had closed the front door, Meg said, "Mom, I told the truth when I said I don't remember what the man said the words were." She drew a deep breath.

"Of course," Mom said. "We never would have thought anything else."

Meg nodded quickly in response to Mom, but it was obvious that she had something else to say. After another pause she added, "But I wrote them down."

CHAPTER 2

Don't Call Us— We'll Call You

"You wrote down the words the man told you?" Mom asked.

"Uh-huh," Meg said, moving her head up and down in quick, small nods.

"Where did you write it down?" asked Brandon.

"In the kitchen," answered Meg.

Brandon let out an exasperated sigh. "No, I mean what did you write it down on? Where is it?"

Meg just stared at Brandon. Before she could answer, Dad asked her, "Why didn't you say anything when the men were here?"

"Two reasons," said Meg, glancing sideways and back again.

"What reasons?" asked Dad.

"The first reason is," Meg paused, "I don't know where it is."

"What?" Brandon asked.

"I don't remember what I wrote it on!" Meg said.

"Well, you haven't looked for it yet, have you?" asked Mom. "You just barely remembered it when the men were here, right?"

"No," said Meg. "I thought about it when Dad came home that day. I tried to find it, but I couldn't."

"Where did you look?" asked Dad.

"*Everywhere!*" said Meg, holding her palms up. "And I looked for it again yesterday, because I thought about it again yesterday."

We all just stared at her.

"I don't know what I did with it," said Meg.

"Are you sure you don't remember what it said?" asked Brandon.

"No," said Meg, looking a little indignant. "I told the truth. I didn't lie."

"We know you didn't lie," said Mom, pulling her close and hugging her.

"What's the other reason?" I asked. "You said there were two reasons why you didn't tell the men that you wrote it down."

Meg paused. She looked like she wasn't sure how to say what she was thinking.

"You can say it," Dad encouraged her. "It's okay."

She paused another moment before saying, "Because somebody told me to wait."

"Wait, what?" said Shauna.

"Who told you to wait?" asked Dad.

"I don't know," Meg confessed. "A man."

"When was that?" asked Mom.

"Right when I was about to say something to the FBI men," said Meg, "I heard a man's voice."

Dad looked surprised. "You heard a voice?"

Meg nodded silently. Then she said, "The voice said, 'Wait until you find it.'"

"Until you find your paper?" asked Mom.

"I think so," said Meg. "I think that's what he meant."

Dad's eyebrows pulled up high and he scratched his head.

Mom said, "You did the right thing, Meg. You answered all their questions and you didn't have anything more to tell them that would have helped. When we find the paper, then we'll call and tell them about it, okay?"

Meg smiled and snuggled in closer to Mom. She seemed to relax a little as she let out a small sigh and said, "Okay. Thanks."

Dad looked like he was still trying to figure it out. "You're right," he said finally. "It made no difference that she didn't say anything."

Looking at Meg, he asked, "And the voice said to wait to tell them until you had found it, right?"

Meg pushed her lips together and nodded.

Dad seemed satisfied with that. "All right," he said. "Shall we see if we can find it now?"

Meg suddenly looked tired, but she agreed to try once more. We all spent about an hour looking through everything we could think of. We searched through stacks of mail and papers in the kitchen, where she had been when she wrote it down. We searched her bedroom. We looked between magazines and books in the family room.

Mom and Dad have this crazy method of cleaning up the kitchen counter when people are coming over: they will just scoop everything into a big, brown paper bag, write the date on it, and put the bag in the closet in the office. We went through two or three paper bags like that and everything else in the office. But we couldn't find the message.

The biggest problem was that we didn't really even know what we were looking for. Meg couldn't remember what she had written it on. The words could have been on anything from a little sticky note to a legal size pad of yellow paper—or even something else. Meg felt bad about having lost the paper, but everyone seemed pretty okay with it, really.

Personally, I thought Meg was amazing. She had really changed a lot in the last year or so. She seemed a lot more like a real person now, instead of just a little girl. The coolest thing was that she had discovered how much fun it is to read. I'm sure that in the last year alone, she has read more books than I *ever* have, even though I'm five years older! A couple times a month she'd beg Mom to take her to the public library to check out more books. Each time she went, she would get five or six books that were at least a couple hundred pages each. Mom would only let her check out as many as she could carry, otherwise I'm sure she would have come home with more. As soon as she got out to the car, she would always put them right into her pink backpack. This backpack had been her constant companion for over a year now—ever since she got it. At first she carried some crazy things in it, but now it was used almost exclusively for books.

She did something really funny, though. She would rarely read an entire book straight through. Instead, she would be in various stages of reading three or four books at one time. I don't know how she kept it all straight! And another thing that's amazing is that she would *never* use a bookmark! When she went back to a book, she would just thumb through the pages for a moment or two, reading here and there until she found her spot again. What a smart kid!

The day before we were to leave on our trip, Dad took the day off from work so that he could help get everything ready. Agent Tassel-Shoes had called every single day to see if we had any more information or if Meg had remembered anything else the man on the phone had told her. He seemed to be getting more intense each time he called. By this time, no one except for Mom and Dad would answer the phone anymore, because none of the rest of us wanted to talk to him—especially Meg.

The night before we were going to leave, we all gathered around the kitchen table for a family devotional. It was Chelsea's turn to pick the song, so we sang "I Love to See the Temple," then Danny said the prayer.

"Who knows what tomorrow is?" Mom asked.

"Saturday," said Danny. "I know 'cause earlier in the week you said that we're leaving on Saturday and today you said that we're leaving tomorrow!"

"That's right, Daniel," said Mom. "Good job."

Danny looked around the table at everyone to see if we all agreed that he had done a good job.

"But what else is tomorrow?" Mom asked.

Danny quickly returned his gaze to Mom, with a look that said he couldn't believe there might be something else.

"The second Saturday in July?" asked Brandon.

"Yes," Mom answered, "but what else?"

Danny, who was sitting next to Brandon, leaned close to him and loudly whispered, "Mom didn't say that *you* did a good job."

"Good job, Brandon," Mom said quickly, looking straight at Danny, "but what else is tomorrow?"

"Oh, I know," smiled Shauna. "It's the second Saturday of the month, the day you and Dad usually do genealogy."

"Right," said Mom.

Mom and Dad liked doing genealogy. They tried to go to the family history center the second Saturday of each month and would usually take one of us with them. A couple times a year, we would all go to the temple and do baptisms for the dead. It was really kind of fun. I think Dad's genealogy was all pretty much done by his grandparents, but there was still a lot to do on Mom's side.

"Since we're leaving on our trip first thing in the morning and tomorrow can't be a genealogy day," Mom continued, "we decided to have a genealogy devotional today. Does anyone remember who Elias Franzen is?"

"Is he one of our grandfathers with lots of 'greats' in front?" asked Chelsea.

"What do you mean?" laughed Dad.

"I mean like great-great-grandfather," said Chelsea, "or great-great-great-great-grandfather or something like that."

"I think it's three greats," said Brandon.

"That's right," agreed Mom. Then she asked, "And did you know that we're going to a place where he lived?"

"We *are?*" asked Chelsea with excitement.

"Where?" asked Meg.

"Kirtland, Ohio," said Mom.

"Didn't a lot of Church things happen there?" I asked.

"Yes," said Mom. "The headquarters of the Church were in

16

Kirtland from 1831 to 1838, so a lot of things happened there. Does anyone remember anything specific?"

"There was a temple there," I said.

"It was the very first temple," said Meg. I looked at her in surprise, wondering how she would know that. Maybe she was reading even more than I thought she was.

"Is it still there?" Chelsea asked. "Or is it gone now?"

"It's still there," said Mom, "but it's not owned by our Church."

"Isn't it owned by the Reorganized Church?" Shauna asked.

"Right," said Dad, "but they've changed their name to the Community of Christ."

"Does anyone remember anything else that happened in Kirtland?" Mom asked.

After a pause, Dad said, "I know that many of the revelations in the Doctrine and Covenants were received in Kirtland—but I don't remember how many."

"Great," Mom said. "Let's all look in the index of the triple combination and see what we can find."

As we all opened our books and started turning pages, Mom said, "Look up the word *Kirtland* and anything associated with it."

We soon found that there were headings for both *Kirtland, Ohio*, and *Kirtland Temple*.

Under the first heading was a listing of all the revelations in the Doctrine and Covenants that were received in Kirtland. Dad counted them up and said, "Whoa! It looks like 46 of them. I think I read somewhere that of all the sections in the Doctrine and Covenants, there were more revelations received in Kirtland than in any other place. I believe it!"

"Oh, I remember talking about the Kirtland Temple in seminary," said Brandon. "It's where the sealing power was restored, too, wasn't it? We studied the Doctrine and Covenants last year."

"You're right," smiled Mom.

"What's the sealing power?" asked Danny.

"That's the power that keeps husbands and wives and families together forever," said Dad.

"Does anyone know where we can read about it?" asked Mom.

We all scanned through the references in the index of each of our books.

"Here it is," I said. "Didn't it happen as part of the visions? Under *Kirtland Temple* it says *sec. 110 visions received in.*"

We turned to Section 110 of the Doctrine and Covenants and read the whole thing out loud, listing everyone who visited Joseph Smith and Oliver Cowdery in the Kirtland Temple that day: Jehovah (who is Jesus Christ), Moses, Elias, and Elijah. In verse 14 we read that Elijah told them, "Behold, the time has fully come, which was spoken of by the mouth of Malachi."

And then in verse 15 it says, "To turn the hearts of the fathers to the children, and the children to the fathers, lest the whole earth be smitten with a curse—"

"Elijah gave them the sealing power," explained Mom. "That's what seals us together in families." Then she asked, "Does anyone have any idea why the sealing power was restored at this time?"

We all just stared at her.

"What had just happened?" she continued. "Look at the section right before this one: Section 109."

"It's the prayer from the dedication of the temple," said Brandon. "So the temple had just been dedicated."

"Oh, right," nodded Shauna. "Look at the dates of the two sections. The dedication happened on March twenty-seventh and the visions on April third. Joseph Smith received several visions in the temple right after it was dedicated."

"It was exactly one week later," smiled Dad. "Any idea what was important about Elijah coming on April third?"

Nobody had an answer. Dad tried to help us along by asking, "Does anyone remember what the Jews are expecting Elijah to do?"

"Oh, yeah!" Shauna said. "He's supposed to return during

Passover, isn't he? Don't they set an extra place at the table for him?"

"Right," Dad said. "It could just be an empty chair, or an extra glass—each family might do it a little differently—but the point is that they know that he is supposed to return during Passover. And April third was during Passover that year."

Mom added, "And Elijah brought the sealing power to Joseph Smith and Oliver Cowdery. Now where do we perform sealing ordinances?"

"In the temple!" said Chelsea.

"Exactly," smiled Mom. "So as soon as there was a place to perform the ordinances, they received the authority to do it!"

We all nodded our understanding. Just when we thought we knew it all, Mom asked, "What else is needed, besides the temple and the authority to perform sealing ordinances?"

We all stared at her, showing absolutely no understanding.

"What was the first thing that the Lord told Lehi to send his sons back for?" asked Mom.

"R-r-records?" Brandon said, with obvious uncertainty. He glanced back and forth between Dad and Shauna as he tried to decide whether or not to say the whole word.

"Right," nodded Mom, "and what was included with the records that Nephi brought back to his father, Lehi?"

"The sword of Laban!" I said, remembering one of my favorite stories.

Mom laughed a little and then rephrased her question. "What was written *as part of* the records?" she asked.

We all stared blankly again. Finally, Dad helped us by asking, "What are we *not* going to be able to do tomorrow?"

"Genealogy!" said Chelsea, obviously pleased to be the first one to get the answer. She wriggled up taller in her chair.

"Oh, that's right," Shauna said, "there was a genealogy of Lehi's forefathers."

19

There was a pause. Mom was just smiling, obviously waiting for more. Finally Brandon asked what we were all wondering, "What was the question again?"

"What do we need besides the temple and the authority?" Mom repeated.

"Oh, yeah," Shauna laughed. "We need the names of people who need the ordinances!"

"That's right," said Mom. "The first time we go to the temple, we perform ordinances for ourselves, but from then on we perform them for others. That's why we do genealogy, so that we can perform temple ordinances and be sealed to our ancestors and they to us."

Mom had us all turn to the fifth chapter of 1 Nephi and read the part where Lehi discovers his genealogy. He learned from the records that he was a descendant of Joseph, who had been sold into Egypt.

Then we looked in the index again under the reference *Temple*. We found that one of the first things that Nephi did was build a temple. It was modeled after Solomon's temple, which is described in the Old Testament. We looked up all the scriptures in the Book of Mormon about temples. We decided that the temple is also a place for teaching, because so many of the prophets went there to teach. Jacob did, and so did King Benjamin. When Christ appeared to the people in the Americas after his resurrection in Jerusalem, he came to the temple. And it was at the temple that he taught them and blessed them.

"Did Elias Franzen do his temple ordinances in the Kirtland Temple?" Meg asked. Her question reminded me where the devotional started. "He's the one you said lived in Kirtland, right?"

"Yes, he lived there," said Mom, "but his ordinances weren't done until his family lived in Nauvoo and the Nauvoo Temple was done."

"Did Hannah live in Kirtland, too?" I asked.

Hannah was Elias Franzen's daughter. The old Book of Mormon that Brandon got from our Great-aunt Ella had been given to Hannah by her father at the time they left Nauvoo to go west. There was some really old writing inside the front cover of the book. It was a note to Hannah, signed "D." Aunt Ella said she thought that was short for *Dad* or *Daddy*, because that's what Hannah always called him.

"I don't think Hannah lived in Kirtland," said Mom, answering my earlier question.

"I think Elias moved from Kirtland to Missouri before Hannah was born," Dad added.

"But," said Mom with a smile, "we're going to do something really fun in Kirtland. There is a family history center there where they have a listing of everyone who was living in Kirtland at the time the Church had its headquarters there."

"Did Elias Franzen live there then?" I asked.

"Yes," answered Mom, "and so we're going to find out whatever we can about him while we're there. I think it's going to be a lot of fun."

Everyone agreed. Everyone except Danny, that is.

"I think Danny's tired," Brandon said.

We all looked over at him and saw that he was face down on the table with his forehead against his open book. When the silence in the kitchen was broken by his quiet snore, we all burst out laughing.

"I can't believe how fast that kid can fall asleep!" I laughed.

"And *where!*" Shauna agreed.

"I know," said Brandon. "Remember when we couldn't find him for dinner one night until we looked inside the old dishwasher box in the basement? The box was so flat I thought it was empty!"

"At least until we heard him snore," giggled Meg.

We all laughed again, then Mom said she thought it was time to be done with our devotional.

"It's a good thing Danny said the opening prayer," Dad smiled. "I'll say the closing prayer."

The next day turned out to be a pretty normal day. We had all been on airplanes the previous two summers, so there wasn't much that was new or unexpected for everyone. Danny did comment when we were flying through a bunch of fluffy, white clouds that he didn't remember seeing the "Cotton Candy Land" before.

We flew from Salt Lake City to Cincinnati, where we had to change planes. We were in the airport for less than an hour, but Dad let us each choose what we wanted to eat before we went back to get on the plane again. It turned out to be a good thing, since we didn't get anything to eat on the airplane from Cincinnati except for peanuts and soda. After we landed in Cleveland, we took a shuttle bus to the rental place and picked up our van. Dad was right: it was *exactly* like our van at home. It was even the exact same color: boring white—top to bottom and front to back, there was nothing but a whole lot of white.

From the airport it was about a forty-minute drive to our hotel where we checked into a two-bedroom suite that was really nice. It even had a full kitchen. Shauna and Meg got to share the bed in the small bedroom, with Chelsea on a roll-away bed. Brandon and I got to share the queen-size sofa bed in the main family room area that was joined with the kitchen. We were both pleased that we wouldn't need to go very far for midnight snacks. Danny was going to sleep on a roll-away bed in the large bedroom where Mom and Dad would be sleeping. There were two bathrooms, too, but you had go through one of the bedrooms to get to them, so it was a pain for me and Brandon.

It was in our suite that Meg made an interesting discovery. We were all just about finished unpacking when Meg rushed out of the bedroom yelling, "I found it! I found it!"

"Found what?" Dad asked, looking up from the suitcase he was unpacking.

She giggled as she held up a paper and said, "I found the message from the man. I was using it as a bookmark!"

"But you never use bookmarks!" I said in disbelief. I came over to where she was standing.

"I know," she giggled again. "But this book was not as interesting as all the other books I was reading, so I knew that I wouldn't get back to it for a while. So I thought I would try it for once—'cause I know some people really like using bookmarks."

We all just stared at her. She wrinkled up her nose and said, "But I forgot that I did it. Sorry!" She giggled again.

I'm sure my mouth was wide open for several moments before I finally started saying, "After all that time we spent . . ." Mom threw a quick glare in my direction that stopped me mid-sentence with my mouth still open.

"Who cares?" said Brandon. "What does it say?"

"Do you want me to read it?" Meg asked with sparkling eyes.

"That would be great," Dad smiled.

Meg shifted her weight back and forth on her feet a couple of times and read the message out loud to us: "This man found these faded words along edge of paper: 'Dear Hannah, Carry on efforts to assure that B. Wright retrieved his funds from my Kirtland home. Love, -D.'"

No one said anything, so Meg added. "I didn't know the right way to spell *Wright* until he told me, so I changed it to be right."

Brandon looked a little confused by her comment. Then he shook his head slightly, as if to get it out of his brain before saying, "Hannah? That's another note to Hannah from her dad, Elias Franzen?"

"Certainly sounds like it," Mom agreed. "May I look at it, Meg?" she asked.

Meg handed Mom the note and Mom and Dad both read it a couple more times.

"What does it mean?" asked Mom.

"I have no idea," Dad admitted, "but we had better call the FBI agent and tell him about it."

"Now?" Mom asked.

"Well, he said to call as soon as we found anything," said Dad.

Dad immediately went and got the business card that Agent Fashion Show had given him. He pushed some buttons on the phone and waited, holding Meg's bookmark in his hand.

"Agent Smith," Dad said after a moment. "This is Craig Andrews." There was a short pause.

"Yes, she found it," Dad said, nodding his head at the phone base on the table. "That's why I'm calling." Another short pause.

"Of course," Dad said. Then he started reading into the phone, "'Dear Hannah, Carry on efforts to ensure that B. Wright retrieved his funds'—oh, you're right—'assure that B. Wright retrieved his funds from my Kirtland home. Love, -D.'" Dad waited for just a moment before asking, "How did you know that?"

Now there was a much longer pause before Dad said, "I see."

Another pause. "All right. Thanks for your time."

Dad hung up and looked around at us with a really weird, confused look on his face.

"What's going on?" asked Mom.

Dad waited a moment before answering. Then he said, "The agent acted really strange."

"Like how?" I asked.

"Well," Dad said slowly. "First of all, when I read the note wrong, he corrected me. At first I said 'ensure' and then he said 'assure' to me while I was still reading it."

"Really?" said Mom.

"Yeah," nodded Dad slowly. "But when I asked him how he knew, he said it was just a guess, because *assure* sounded more like the type of word that would have been used. Then he said that he had lots of experience dealing with documents and writings from this time period."

"How odd," Mom said.

"I know," Dad said. "I didn't really say much, because I thought it sounded pretty far-fetched."

"Who would believe *that?*" I said to no one in particular. Brandon and Shauna looked like they both were thinking the same thing.

"Get this," Dad continued. "Then he told me that it sounded like a dead end, thanked me for my time, and told me not to worry about it anymore. I think he was about to hang up when he blurted out something like I shouldn't put too much stock in the word *funds* either, because at that time, it could have easily meant something like crops or chickens. Then he laughed really funny and said something about all the chickens being dead a long time ago."

Mom looked at Dad like it was the strangest thing she'd ever heard. "And that was all?" she asked.

"The last thing he said was, 'Don't call us, we'll call you'," Dad said. "I got the distinct impression that he already had a copy of the message and that he wished I had never found it."

"Is that true about the word *funds?*" I asked.

"I don't know," Dad confessed. "I sure wish I had my dictionary."

CHAPTER 3

Elias Franzen's Home

We talked for a while about the FBI agent's weird response to Dad's phone call, then decided we should get something to eat. It was already late evening, so we went to a family restaurant across the street. They were closing for the night, but Mom and Dad asked just about every employee in the restaurant where we would be able to find the "best grocery store." It turned out that everyone had a different opinion about what "best" meant. I have no idea what the employees thought, but I think Mom was thinking "lots of choices" and Dad was thinking "cheap." Eventually we found something that Mom and Dad could agree on.

We would be staying in the same place for five days, so they bought enough food for all day Sunday, breakfast each of the other days, snacks for the van, and some other stuff for anytime we happened to be back at the room and wouldn't be eating out. I was hoping that wouldn't be too often.

It was late by the time we got back to the hotel, but I don't think even one of us was very tired. We had lost two hours because of the time zone change. Dad wanted us to go to sleep, though, because we were going to church in a ward in Kirtland the next morning at 10:00, which would feel like 8:00 for us. Dad tried to get us to go to bed, but he failed. None of us minded until he woke us up in the morning and kept telling us to hurry, since we had eight people sharing two bathrooms.

26

Dad is too organized for his own good. He is *so* organized that he ends up thinking that everything should work perfectly. Then, on those "rare" occasions when things don't run quite the way he thinks they should, he gets a weird combination of flustered and depressed. That makes it worse, because he convinces himself that if he had been even *more* organized, everything would have worked. It's a vicious cycle.

Here's an example. In preparation for our trip Dad spent hours on the Internet, printing pages to go into a blue three-ring binder that had everything from maps to reservation numbers. He had complete information about every hotel we were going to be staying in. He had a separate map for every place we might be visiting— complete with detailed directions and time estimates from the hotel where we were staying as well as every other place we might possibly be visiting that day. He had all the maps and reservations for each day organized in his blue binder with those little colored divider pages.

According to one of Dad's Internet maps, the "total estimated time" for us to get from our hotel to the church building was 13 minutes. So Sunday morning, Dad tried to have everyone ready by 9:30 so that when we drove the estimated 13 minutes to church, we would still be about 15 minutes early. It didn't happen. We didn't even pull out of the hotel parking lot until about 9:45. As much as Dad hates being late for church, he can't seem to justify breaking the speed limit to get there on time. My soccer coach would tell him he "just doesn't want it bad enough."

With Dad driving as quickly and carefully (and legally) as possible, and with Mom in the seat next to him reading the directions from the map, we arrived at exactly 9:59 at the Kirtland Country Club—a private golf course. Dad was devastated. After two U-turns within about 100 yards of each other (because the directions *had* to be correct), we were both officially lost and officially late. After two more U-turns, we were now five minutes late and far closer to a

27

round of golf than to a sacrament tray. Gratefully, Mom had her cellular phone with her and, using Dad's trusty, blue three-ring binder of phone numbers and addresses for every place we would even think about visiting on this vacation, she called the church. Luckily, someone answered the phone. They informed us that we were a quarter of a mile away and on the wrong side of the road. So much for the Internet directions.

We made it in time for the sacrament, but Dad was depressed about the apparent failure of his blue notebook for much of the rest of the day. I'm sure he was trying to figure out how he could have been more organized. I was worried that he might start making us do a dry run for every place where we had to be at a certain time. He is such an extremist, though, I also feared that he might just throw the book out completely and simply drive in circles for the next ten days, all the while mumbling about this being better than depending on the undependable.

After church Dad said, "Most of the historical sites and the visitors' center are just down the road. Shall we go there now?"

I was wondering if he had already forgotten about the getting-to-church disaster when I asked, "You're not going by the same directions that took us to the golf course instead of sacrament meeting, are you?"

Dad, in an effort to remain calm, chose not to answer me right away, instead plastering a smile on his face that I took to mean *I forgive you*. That gave me an excellent opportunity to see just how far I could push it. After all, at a recent family night Dad had reminded us that Jesus taught us to forgive seventy times seven.

"We made so many U-turns," I continued, "that I was getting dizzy."

Brandon laughed and so I felt encouraged. "How many U-turns will we have to make before we get to the visitors' center?" I asked.

Mom looked over at Dad as though she agreed that it was a valid question.

"As many as necessary," Dad said calmly.

"Oh," I smiled, "so you see U-turns as part of the fun of following bad directions?"

"Whatever it takes to get us to our ultimate destination," Dad smiled back.

I thought the words *ultimate destination* made him sound like a karate or kung fu teacher or something, so with my best Chinese accent I said, "Ah! Master U! We be most happy to follow in many circle to get to *nowhere*." At the same time I spoke, I began bending forward and back from the waist, with my hands pressed flat together in front of me.

At first I had my eyes closed, but then Brandon whacked me on the arm and said, copying my Chinese accent, "Look eye! Always look eye!" So I stared into Dad's eyes as I continued to bend forward and back. He looked like he didn't know how to respond, so I said, "The great Master U take us to ultimate destination with many U-turns!"

By this time, I think the rest of the kids were laughing. Even Mom seemed to be enjoying it. I couldn't be sure of everyone's reaction though, because I continued to "look eye" with Dad.

Finally, Dad said, "I asked one of the members and he told me where the visitors' center is. I don't think it will require any 'U-turns!'"

"I'm sure you're right," Mom smiled—then her smile quickly changed to desperation as she added, "but I'm starving!"

"Me, too!" Chelsea whined. Danny and Meg quickly chimed in, followed by the rest of us, and Dad soon saw that he was outnumbered. The reason we were all starving was because, obviously, none of us had gotten up in time to eat any breakfast. And none of us stopped long enough to think about bringing something out to the van to eat on the way. Why we didn't just leave the stuff in the van when we came home from the store, I don't know. But Dad finally

29

agreed that we could return to the hotel to eat lunch and change clothes.

Dad wanted to go back to Kirtland as soon as we were done eating so we could start touring some of the Church sites, but he got outvoted once again. After a plane ride that was too long and boring, followed by too little sleep, waking up too early, too many unfamiliar people at church, and too much lunch, the rest of us were just too tired. All we wanted to do was lay around and sleep. So that's what we did. Except Dad, of course. I think he spent the next couple of hours reading every brochure available from the lobby, followed by an in-depth study of his blue binder.

By the time the rest of us woke up from our naps, Dad was raring to go. We piled into the van to head back to Kirtland, only this time with a *healthy* supply of snacks—I mean healthy in the massive, sumo-wrestler sense, not necessarily in the good-for-you, high-fiber, lots-of-fruits-and-vegetables sense.

It turned out that Dad was right about how close the church had been to the visitors' center and some other sites. We got there without any U-turns. But since I had been calling him "Master U" the entire way there, he decided to play along. He made two U-turns in the nearly empty parking lot before finally choosing a parking spot and turning off the engine. He turned to me and said with absolutely no feeling in his voice, "Hop out now, grasshopper."

We spent the next couple of hours watching a video in the visitors' center and then walking around to a bunch of buildings. The Newell K. Whitney store was still mostly original, but the Church had restored Joseph and Emma's home, the John Johnson Inn, and a building they called an "ashery." One of my favorite places was the water-driven sawmill. There were missionaries everywhere telling us all about everything. It was cool to learn how much of the early Church history happened here, and to see the room above the Newell K. Whitney store where the School of the Prophets was held and where Joseph Smith received so many revelations.

We had wanted to stop in at the family history center to learn more about Elias Franzen, but it was closed on Sundays. Mom and Dad said that we would come back the next day, since Dad still had several pages in his blue binder listing things to see in the Kirtland area.

By then, we had been walking around for hours and were all starving again. We couldn't wait to get back in the van and the food we had stashed there. But that just turned out to be torture. Mom wouldn't let us eat anything. She said, "I have absolutely no intention of wasting my time making supper for a bunch of kids who just tanked up all the way home."

We groaned as much as we dared, but she wouldn't give in. It turned out to be a pretty good strategy, though, because we were all anxious to help get dinner ready just so we could eat as soon as possible. I guess that's the kind of thing you learn after years of experience being a mom.

Monday morning Dad let us sleep in. I think he was hoping we wouldn't be as grouchy as we had been the day before.

"Where are we going?" Danny asked as we approached the van.

"The first place we want to go," said Mom, "is the family history center."

"What's that?" asked Danny.

"That's where we learn about the people we are related to who lived a long time ago," Mom explained.

As I slid the door open and started to climb inside the van, Dad said, "Hey, wasn't it locked?"

No one said anything for a moment, until Meg admitted, "Maybe I forgot to lock it again when I came out last night to get my book."

Dad stared blankly back at her. "Okay," he finally said. "Everyone think about what you left in here yesterday and make sure that it's all still here."

Brandon and I checked out all the food and were pleased to find

31

that each of our favorites was still present and accounted for. Dad was the only one who seemed to think anything was missing.

"Where's my blue binder?" he said to no one in particular. "I had it under the seat." He looked up and said to everyone, "Has anyone seen it? Will you look around, please?"

We looked around, but it was nowhere to be found.

"Did you maybe leave it in the room?" Mom asked.

Dad was sure he hadn't, but he returned to our hotel room and searched anyway. Ten minutes later he came back, looking slightly discouraged.

"It's not there," he said.

"I'm sorry," Meg said. "I should have locked it."

"Don't worry about it," Dad said with a sad smile. "I always say that if it's important, we shouldn't leave it in the car, don't I? So if it's lost, it's my own fault."

We drove pretty much in silence to the family history center. Mom went inside, and we all followed right behind her, with Dad bringing up the rear—after making sure the van was locked.

"I understand you have information about everyone who was living in Kirtland during the 1830s," Mom said to the lady at the desk.

"That's correct," she smiled back.

"My great-great-grandfather is named Elias Franzen," Mom said. "I believe he was living here at that time."

"How do you spell the last name?" the lady asked, as she began typing on a computer keyboard.

Mom spelled *Franzen* for her and we all waited for a few moments.

"Here he is," the lady said. "It looks like he was living here when Joseph Smith arrived in early 1831, but he left with a group of Saints for Missouri in July of that same year."

She turned to us and said, "So he wasn't here for too much of the time that we have records for, but there's no telling how long he was here before that."

"What else do you have about him?" Mom asked.

The lady turned back to the computer screen and said, "Well, he was baptized in May, just two months before leaving for Missouri." Looking up from her screen, she said, "There were quite of few of the local townspeople baptized here in those first few months after Joseph Smith arrived."

She turned back to the screen and scanned over the information for a moment before saying, "Oh, here's something interesting. It looks like the home that he lived in is still standing."

"Really?" Mom asked. "Do you have the address?"

The lady looked up at her and said, "Now you understand that it's not owned by the Church, don't you? There are people living in it now. I'm sure it's alright if you drive by and have a look, but I know they will appreciate having their privacy."

"Of course," Dad said.

The lady gave us the address as well as directions on how to get there. It turned out not to be too far away. It was up the hill.

Dad quickly found the address of Elias Franzen's home and parked across the street. The house was small, but it looked well taken care of. I never would have guessed that it was nearly two hundred years old. It was two stories tall with a small porch in front. There was a large yard on all sides with huge trees around the edges.

"Shall we get out and take a closer look?" Dad asked.

"I thought we weren't supposed to bother them," I said.

"I don't plan on bothering anybody," Dad said, turning around in his seat at the same time he pushed the van door open. "I'm just going to walk along the sidewalk. Do you want to come?"

"I do," yelled Danny, who still went everywhere he could, any time he had the chance.

"Can I come?" Chelsea asked.

Soon everyone had piled out and began crossing the narrow,

empty road. I walked down the street a little before crossing in an attempt to avoid being part of the long line that everyone else was making. They looked like a family of ducks.

Dad spent the next few minutes pointing out interesting things about the house. It was covered with wood siding, but Dad said it probably wasn't the original. The windows were all pretty small and he had us all stand in a certain spot so we could see how wavy and uneven the old glass was. We also looked at the various colored stones that were used to make the foundation. As we started back across the road to leave, an old man opened the squeaky screen door and came out onto the cracked sidewalk that ran from the front door to the edge of the road. He was wearing a Cleveland Indians baseball hat, a plaid shirt with flaps over each of the two pockets on his chest, dark blue jeans that were held in place with an old, leather belt, and very white tennis shoes that looked like they had just come out of the box.

"What d' ya think of this old house?" he asked, as the screen door slammed. He stuck his thumbs inside his belt by his hips.

"Hello," Mom answered. "We think it's beautiful."

"Lived here all m' life," the man smiled with satisfaction, as he sauntered closer to the road. He threw a contented glance over his shoulder.

"Wow," Dad smiled. "You've taken very good care of the place. It looks very nice."

"Thank you," nodded the man. Then, reaching his hand out toward Dad, he said, "Rudy's the name. How do you do?"

"Nice to meet you," Dad said, shaking Rudy's hand. "I'm Craig and this is my wife, Sarah."

"I hope we didn't disturb you," Mom explained, "but we just discovered that my great-great-grandfather lived in this home and so we just stopped to take a look."

"Well, c'mon inside and get the whole view," Rudy said, gesturing toward the house with a flick of his head.

"Are you sure?" Mom asked.

"Sure I'm sure," Rudy said with a nod and a click of his tongue. Then he added, "The Missus just adores any opportunity she can get to dote on some young 'uns. Are they all yours?"

"Thank you," Dad said. "Yes, they are."

Rudy wanted to know what our names were. With the open screen door pressing against his backside, he shook each of our hands as we went into the small home.

"Meet the Missus," Rudy said as an elderly woman came into the parlor where we stood, wiping her hands with a small towel. Her well-worn slippers shuffled on the wood floor until she reached the large rug that filled most of the room. She was wearing long pants, a flowered blouse, and an old apron covered with faded pictures of apples, strawberries, and other fruits.

"Hello," she smiled, reaching for Mom's hand. "I'm Chloe."

"It's very nice to meet you," Mom said, reaching to shake Chloe's hand. "I'm Sarah and this is my husband, Craig."

"Are these your children?" Chloe asked.

"Yes," smiled Mom, and we were all introduced.

"Sarah's granddaddy lived here," Rudy said to Chloe.

"Really?" said Chloe, with obvious pleasure at the thought.

"Actually, he was my great-great-grandfather," Mom explained.

"A granddaddy is a granddaddy," smiled Chloe. "Family is family. It doesn't matter how close they are related or how far—we love 'em all just the same, don't we?"

Turning to me and Brandon, Chloe said, "Now I'm sure I can get a couple of pieces of fresh peach pie down each of you, can't I?"

I hesitated, glancing at Mom first.

Chloe said with a smile, "There's nothing quite like fresh pie on a late summer morning to hold you through till lunchtime."

Mom smiled and nodded at me, so I quickly said, "Yes! Of course!"

Brandon added, "Sure!"

"And the rest of you, too?" Chloe asked, looking from person to person.

"Uh-huh," giggled Meg. Shauna just smiled and nodded.

"I can see you are smart children," Chloe said with determination. She turned and shuffled back into the kitchen, saying, "Come sit around the table."

As we followed Chloe, Rudy gestured toward the sofa in the parlor and said to Dad, "Have a seat."

As Dad started to sit, Mom said, "I think I'll help Chloe in the kitchen."

I can honestly say that was the best peach pie I have ever tasted. The top crust was flaky and covered with a sugary glaze. The inside was sweet and juicy. After serving us at the table, Chloe and Mom took plates into the parlor for the four of them. We could hear them talking about all sorts of things as we ate our pie. We mostly just talked about how good the pie was and how nice Rudy and Chloe were.

Fifteen or twenty minutes later, we had rinsed our plates off in the sink and were sitting at the table again, when Dad stuck his head in from the parlor and said, "C'mon, kids. It's time to go."

We pushed our chairs under the table again and followed him toward the door.

"It's been right nice meeting you," said Rudy to Dad. Then he turned to Mom and said, "Now when was it your granddaddy lived in this old place?"

Mom said, "It was in the early 1830s."

Rudy seemed a bit surprised by her answer. After a hesitation, he said, "What was his name?"

"Elias Franzen," answered Mom.

Rudy's eyes narrowed and he looked closely at Mom. "*Franzen* did you say?"

Mom nodded, "That's right."

Rudy paused briefly and then said, "Hold on a minute. I have something to show you."

He went into the kitchen and returned a moment later with a yellowish paper in his hand.

"We had the floors redone in here a couple of months back," said Rudy. "And the feller who did it wanted to pull off the baseboards around the bottom of all the walls so that he could sand the floor all the way to the edge. It looked to me like those boards were as old as the house."

Holding the paper out toward Dad where we could all get a good look at it, he said, "We found this behind one of the baseboards. It looked like it had been there for a long time." The paper was folded in thirds and sealed with a drop of dark red wax. Above the wax, written in old handwriting were the words:

To B. Wright.

From E. Franzen, July 1831.

CHAPTER 4

B. Wright

Dad carefully turned the paper over in his hands a couple of times.

"We wondered about it," said Rudy. "We thought about opening it, but it just didn't seem right."

"It's not ours," explained Chloe. "And if that date is correct, then it belongs to the next of kin. But as far as we could tell, we aren't related to anyone named either *Wright* or *Franzen*."

"But it sounds like *you folks* are," Rudy added.

Dad was just staring at the paper as they spoke. Finally he handed it to Mom and said, "He's only related to me by marriage—he's your double great-grandfather, not mine."

Mom just stared at the paper in her hand.

"I'll open it!" Brandon blurted out. "If he's Mom's double great-grandfather, then that makes him my *triple* great-grandfather." He held his hand out toward Mom, but I don't think she had any intention of handing it over.

"Do you think it was really written by Elias Franzen?" Shauna asked.

"Well," Mom sighed, "we know that he lived in this house until he left for Missouri."

"Didn't the lady say when he moved?" I asked.

"July 1831," Mom nodded. "The exact date of this letter."

"Wow!" Shauna said. "Do you think he wrote a note and left it here when he moved?"

"It seems possible," Dad said.

Brandon started making a noise that sounded really weird and made me look over at him. He looked really strange. His head was starting to twitch and he acted like he was having trouble forcing some words out of his mouth. "So open it!" he finally blurted.

It was so sudden that everyone seemed to jump just a little.

"What are you *waiting* for?" Brandon asked. "We'll *never* know unless we open it!"

"Makes sense to me," Rudy said. "Doesn't seem too likely that either of those fellers will be coming after it." He had a twinkle in his eye.

"Unless he's one of the three Nephites!" I said.

Shauna was the only one who gave any audible response. She guffawed loudly. Dad cringed, and Mom looked like she thought that was a really dumb thing to say. This was the first point at which I realized that what I thought was clever, might not have been the best thing to say in front of people who had no idea what a Nephite was. I looked at Rudy. The twinkle that had been in his eye a moment before was now replaced by confused silence. I could tell he was trying to figure out what I had meant, but his wife saved me.

"You're the nearest thing we can find to a relative of one of them," Chloe said to Mom and Dad.

Taking the opportunity to change the subject with something else clever that could be appreciated by everyone, I said, "Well, hopefully, whatever we do, it will *be right.*" I emphasized the last two words and then said, "Get it? B. Wright?" I made a little fake laugh. "Like the name on the paper?"

Brandon looked annoyed at my comment and said, "Funny, Jeff."

"Alright," Mom said with determination. "Let's open it."

She carefully broke the red wax and unfolded the brittle paper. After glancing briefly over the page from top to bottom, Mom read it out loud for us:

To Blaine Wright, my lifelong friend,

It is already some months since we have had ocasion to share company one with another. I still recollect with some great sadness the discouragement you felt upon your return to Kirtland on April last. It is indeed most unfortunat that the slow sale of your farm in Penn. detained you so long as to prevent you from being here to witness the events which caused the disbanding of The Family that you were keen upon joyning yourself with. Had you witnessed these events first-hand, perhaps your disscouragement would not have been so poignant. Alas, it was not to be and I freely acknowlege the hand of the Almighty in all these doings.

It is my express desire in this correspondance to advise you of the location of the Funds from the sale of your farm that you were forced to leave so hastily in my trust upon your sudden and untimely departure. I had hoped to return them to you in person, but having been called by Brother Joe Smith (leader of the Church of Christ) to make my new home in the state of Missouri, I am persuaded to leave the Funds hidden here that you may regain them immediately upon calling for them.

From the time of our boyhood you may recall the small hyding place that was markt and illuminated thru the attick window at dawn precisely on that day when the sun rises at its latest time all year. Oft have I employed this location for personal treasures and have there cached your Funds from the day they were entrusted to me.

I leave the new owner of my home yet unaware of this situation, rather only with the strictest charge to deliver this correspondance to you at his first opportunity.

God be with you, dear friend, until such time as God sees fit that our paths may once again cross.

E. F.

After at least two full seconds of complete silence, Dad whispered, "Wow!"

"No kidding," said Brandon.

"He must have never come back for his money," said Shauna.

"That's what Meg's note was talking about," I said.

"You're right," agreed Dad. "Elias asked Hannah to keep trying to make sure that his friend got the money—or the funds—whatever they were."

"But if he never got this letter," I said, "then he never would have known where to get it."

"Now aren't you glad you listened to me?" Brandon asked. "And that you read the letter?"

He was pretty much ignored.

"Or maybe the new owner just took the money," I suggested, "and just never bothered to give this letter to this Blaine Wright guy."

"But the wax on the letter was still sealed," Shauna said. "How would he know where the money was?"

"Remember that it might not even be money," Meg said.

"You may have something very valuable hidden in your attic," Dad said to Rudy.

Rudy rubbed his chin and asked, "What do think the chances are that it's still up there?"

"There's been so much remodeling and such that's gone on in here over the years," said Chloe, "I just have a hard time believing that it never was discovered—if it was ever here in the first place."

"Any idea how much money a farm was worth in 1831?" Brandon asked.

"It would depend on the size of the farm," Dad said.

"Well, whatever it was," I said, "it probably isn't hardly anything compared to today."

"That may be true for the total number of dollars," Mom said, "but the money would be worth a lot more than its face value."

41

"What does that mean?" asked Meg.

"What it means is that if you found a five dollar bill that's almost two hundred years old," explained Mom, "then there are dealers and collectors who would probably pay you thousands of dollars for it."

Brandon's eyes got big and he asked, "So if you had a big stack of bills, could you get thousands of dollars for each bill?"

"Of course," Mom said.

"That might be worth at least having a look around for," said Rudy.

"Especially if they're all one dollar bills and no big ones," said Brandon. Then he added, "We'll help you look." Dad sort of glared at him, but I don't think Rudy really noticed what was going on.

"Well, if we want to find this hiding spot," said Rudy, "then we ought to try to figure out what this here means." He pointed to a paragraph in Elias's letter. Reading what he was pointing to, he said, "'Illuminated thru the attic window at dawn precisely on that day when the sun rises at its latest time all year.'"

"That would be the shortest day of the year, wouldn't it?" Shauna asked.

"I would think so," Dad agreed.

"That's December twenty-first, isn't it?" I asked.

"Right," said Dad.

"But a window could mark a pretty big spot," Brandon said.

"I reckon it could," agreed Rudy, thoughtfully. "But the windows up in that attic are fairly small. Would you like to come up and have a look?"

"Oh, Rudy," said Chloe, with a bit of a scowl. "They don't want to be crawling around up there in that dusty, old place."

"Sure we do," said Brandon. Dad threw another glare in his direction.

"Sure they do," Rudy agreed, in a voice that sounded just like Brandon's. "Let's have a look." Brandon smiled back at Dad as if to say, "See!"

"Well, all right," Chloe said with a small sigh, "but let me up there first to make sure it's straight, and everything is out of the way, so's no one gets hurt."

"That's what I like about my wife," said Rudy to Dad. "She's always looking out for everybody else. That's why I married her!"

"I think you made a good choice," smiled Dad.

"No doubt about that," agreed Rudy. "Every year on our anniversary, I look her over and say, 'You're still a keeper.'"

"I'm sure she appreciates that," said Mom with a wry smile.

"And every year," Rudy continued, "she looks back at me and says, 'I'm still not sure about you, yet, but I guess I can put up with you for another year.'"

Mom and Dad both laughed. Brandon and I did, too. Shauna's reaction was unique, though. Her mouth fell open and she made a little whimpering sound.

It had only been a few seconds since Chloe made it to the top of the stairs, but Rudy said, "Well, that's probably been long enough. Let's get on up there before she hollers down for a mop bucket."

He invited our family to go up and he came last. I'm not sure what Chloe thought she might need to straighten up because everything looked really well organized—and packed. It was full of stacks and stacks of boxes, trunks, and a bunch of odds and ends that didn't look like anything I'd ever seen before. There was definitely a lot of stuff, but everything seemed to be in its place. Chloe was right about it being dusty, though. I had to squeeze my nose a couple of times to keep from sneezing. Meg, on the other hand, sneezed at least six times, getting a generous "Bless you!" from Chloe each time. I suggested that she pinch her nose, but she would never try it.

"I apologize for the dust," Chloe said, "but other than that I guess it's not so bad up here."

"Thanks for taking care of us, Sugar," Rudy said to Chloe. Then he turned his attention to one of the walls. "This house is built on an angle," said Rudy. Then he pointed and added, "And that corner of the house points pretty much due east. But, you know," he said thoughtfully, looking around a moment before continuing, "at the time of year we're talking about, the sun comes up more southeast than due east." He walked between a couple of tall stacks of boxes and pointed to a window. "I would reckon that the sun more than likely could only be coming through this window."

"Is there any way to figure out for sure where the sun comes up on December twenty-first or would we just have to wait?" I asked.

"Do you know any celestial people?" asked Chloe.

I was confused by her question, but I hid it well by putting a ridiculous look on my face and saying, "Huh?"

Brandon said with hesitation, "There's . . . this girl at my school . . . that's absolutely . . ."

"Perfect?" I asked.

"Gorgeous!" Brandon said.

"Ha!" I laughed. "I should have known. But I bet I know who you mean!"

"Wait, what?" Shauna said.

Dad laughed. "I don't think either one of you understands what Chloe is asking!" he said.

Dad was still laughing quietly, when Chloe explained, "I'm talking about a person who knows about the solar system and the movement of planets and stars."

"Oh, *that* kind of celestial person," I said. "I thought you meant like . . . never mind what I thought." I shook my head as I spoke. "I know what you mean now."

"We have," said Rudy, putting his thumbs in the sides of his belt again, "a friend who works over at the public library—by the name of Marion."

"Marion knows all about celestial things," said Chloe. "Go to the library and ask for Marion. Do you know where the library is?" she asked. Without waiting for an answer she continued, "Go back out onto Highway 306 where the temple is and from there go about three blocks east. It's on the left."

"Do you want us to pursue this?" asked Mom. "I mean, really, it's your home and after all this time I would think anything in it is *yours*."

"Well, it would be interesting to know what it's all about, but we don't get out much anymore," said Rudy. "Say 'hi' to Marion for us and let us know what you find out."

"If we do find anything," said Chloe, "we can work out the details later."

We all made our way back downstairs and outside. Mom tried to give the letter to Rudy and Chloe, but they insisted that she keep it. She put it carefully inside a pocket in her purse. Thanking them for their kindness and the fresh peach pie, we climbed into the van and drove away.

Dad said, "I guess I had better call the FBI agent about this."

"Do you think so?" Mom asked.

"Don't do it!" I said a lot louder than I meant to. Dad just stared at me in the rearview mirror.

"Didn't he say *not* to call him anymore?" I asked. I was starting to get a bad feeling about that Agent Tassle-Shoes.

"I suppose he did," Dad nodded. "But it just seems that something important like this. . . ." He let his voice trail off.

"Jeff's right," Mom said. "I don't see how this could make a difference to them—and he did tell you not to call."

Dad just nodded again, without saying anything.

"Can we get something to eat?" asked Danny, as we headed up the street.

"No way!" said Brandon, tossing a bag of chips in his direction. "Eat some of those. We're going to the library first. Besides, you just had some pie, didn't you?"

Danny didn't say anything, but just looked with disgust at the bag of chips.

"We're close to the library," said Dad, "so why don't we just stop in there quickly and then go to a restaurant."

Danny agreed and Brandon smiled. But now Meg seemed unhappy. "How quick is quickly?" she asked. "Will I have time to check out some books?"

"*Time* to check out a book—yes," answered Dad. "But we don't really have time to move here so that you can get a library card." He paused before adding, "Most public libraries only let you check things out if you're a resident."

"What's a resident?" Danny asked.

"Someone who lives here," Meg said with disappointment. "Can we ask if we have to live here?"

"Sure," said Mom.

As we drove up the hill toward the library, Chelsea asked, "Is that the temple? I love to see the temple!"

I looked over at her, trying to figure out if she knew she was speaking in Primary-song talk. Before I could say anything, though, Dad answered her question.

"It *is* the temple," he said. "We're going to stop there this afternoon."

We found the library a couple of minutes later and went inside. Since our family is so large, we got the attention of the librarian the moment we walked in the door. He had a pair of glasses perched at the end of his very large nose. They were the funny kind of glasses that looked like they were only the bottom half of bifocals; the curved part that went over his nose was higher than the top of the lenses, which were flat on top and rounded on the bottom.

"May I help you?" he asked.

"Is Marion here?" Mom asked.

"I'm sorry," said the man, "Marion isn't working today but should be here tomorrow. Is there anything that I can help you with?"

"Yes," said Meg. "Do I have to live in Kirtland to check out books?"

"No!" smiled the man. "If you live anywhere in Ohio you can check out library materials."

Meg scrunched her lips together. "We live in Utah," she said.

"Oh," said the man. "I'm sorry. Is there anything else I can help you with?"

"We were told that Marion might help us get some information about planets," said Dad.

"Depending on what you need, I might be able to help," said the man.

"We need to know at what location on the horizon the sun rises on a particular day of the year," Dad explained.

The man looked slightly stunned. "Uhh," he said, "Marion is definitely the one to talk to. Why don't you come back tomorrow?"

Dad thanked him and everyone headed for the door.

"Jeff, come back with me for a minute," Brandon said. I followed him back to the desk where he asked the librarian, "Do you know anything about money from the 1830s?"

The librarian suddenly looked quite interested. "Do you mean United States currency?" he asked.

"Yeah," said Brandon. "How much would a big stack of bills be worth?"

"Quite a bit," said the man slowly. "Each bill could be worth thousands, depending on its condition." Then he asked, "Do you have a big stack of bills like that?"

"We think so," Brandon said. "We're trying to find out."

"Sounds like you're doing some detective work," said the man. "I used to do that sort of thing. I still help out law enforcement people whenever I can."

We just nodded our heads, wondering why he was telling us this.

"If I knew exactly what you had I could be more helpful," said the man.

Outside the library Dad asked Brandon, "You didn't do something silly like ask the man where Marion lives, did you?"

Brandon's face brightened and he stopped dead in his tracks. "Do you think he knows?"

"Probably," said Dad, "but we're not going to ask. And if the guy has any sense, he wouldn't tell us, anyway."

While Brandon pouted, I asked him, "Weren't you in a play once where there was a lady named Marian, the Librarian?"

"Yeah," said Brandon, without interest. He didn't seem to appreciate being distracted from his pout.

"Really?" asked Danny. "Do you think it's the same person?"

There was a moment of stunned silence, because no one was quite sure how to answer his question. So Chelsea took advantage of the break in conversation by asking, "Can we eat now?"

Mom and Dad remembered passing several restaurants between the visitors' center and the freeway. We found a family restaurant and were quickly munching down the free bread they brought out before we ordered. They ended up bringing us at least three more baskets of bread before our food came. When Danny's plate of spaghetti was put in front of him, he said, "I'm not hungry." He was staring at the smiley face on his spaghetti that was made from two meatballs, an olive, and a long, curly carrot strip.

"Maybe you shouldn't have eaten twelve pieces of bread," Brandon suggested.

"But I was *hungry*," Danny moaned. "I'm just not hungry *now*."

"Don't worry about it," Dad cut in. "Just have what you want and we can take the rest with us for later." Danny nodded, but still acted like he thought Brandon should have just minded his own business.

After lunch we went to Isaac Morley's farm. It wasn't too far from the other places that we went to by the visitors' center, but it was probably too far away to walk. There were sister missionaries there who told us about the farm. Apparently there was a group of families living together on the farm that were trying to live what they called "the United Order." They were trying to copy a way of life described in the New Testament where early Christians shared everything with each other. The missionaries said that they "had all things in common." After Joseph Smith came to Kirtland in February 1831, a lot of people joined the Church, including everyone who had been living on Isaac Morley's farm.

When the tour was over, it wasn't until we got to the van that I noticed that Mom wasn't with us. I looked back where we had come from and saw her walking quickly in our direction. I figured she had stayed behind to talk to somebody for a minute. She hardly ever misses an opportunity to talk to people, especially when it's someone she doesn't know. And she usually leaves them laughing. She's amazing that way.

"Hey, guys," Mom said to us as she climbed into the van. "Guess what?"

We waited as she slammed the door.

"I was talking to the senior missionaries," Mom said, "and they told me that if we go down to the John Johnson farm, that there is a restaurant close by where we absolutely *have* to go eat." Looking at a paper in her hand she added, "It's called Mary Yoder's Amish Kitchen, and it's just a few minutes from the farm. They said it's the best food around." Then Mom asked Dad, "Were you planning on going to the John Johnson farm this afternoon?"

"I was planning to go there after we take a tour of the temple," Dad said, "because Joseph and Emma Smith lived at the farm for a while and he received some revelations there—but without my travel book, we'll need to get directions." He sounded a little depressed again as he said that last part.

"She already gave me directions!" Mom beamed. "She said it takes about an hour to get there. So I was thinking that if we go to the temple first, then we could go to the farm and take the tour. By then it will probably be just about time for dinner."

"Sounds good," Dad said. After looking at the directions that

Mom got from the missionaries, he started up the van and drove down the long lane to the road.

"Hey!" Brandon said. "I think I saw that man before."

We all looked toward a small parking lot where a man was walking slowly between a couple of cars and looking around, like he was nervous. He was wearing a yellow straw hat with a wide brim. His long, dark brown hair hung down past his ears and he had a bushy beard. His nose stuck out from under the brim of his hat, but between his hair and beard, that was about all I could make out.

"He looks hot," said Shauna.

"He looks nervous," said Brandon.

"I think so, too," I agreed.

"He looks familiar," Brandon said.

"Well, I imagine," Dad said, "that any Church members in the area are probably all visiting the same places, so it seems pretty likely that you would keep seeing the same people."

We went to the temple and took the tour. It was cool to see the places where Joseph Smith and Oliver Cowdery had seen all those visions that we had read about in our family devotional the day before our trip. When we came out of the building and were walking toward our van, Brandon said, "Hey, look! There's that man again!"

Sure enough, the man was in the parking lot. He was glancing around nervously, just like before. When we started to get closer, he turned and walked quickly through the parking lot and down the sidewalk.

We got in the van and drove down the street in the same direction the guy was walking. He was going a lot slower now.

"Check him out," Brandon said as we drove past. The van had tinted windows, so I figured the guy probably didn't know we were all plastered against the glass, staring at him. He was checking us out, too, though. He didn't turn his head, but his eyes shifted strongly in our direction as we drove past. Then he turned around and walked back in the direction he had come from.

"Do you think he's following us?" asked Brandon.

Dad said, "Well, if we see him at the John Johnson farm, you can ask him, okay?"

"I'm *serious*," Brandon whined.

"So am I!" Dad said.

We didn't see him at the farm. But the tour was really interesting, just like all of the other places. By the time we were done, we were all more than ready to check out this Amish Kitchen restaurant. As for me, I wasn't sure if I was really that hungry, or just tired of walking around and riding in the van. As soon as I started eating, though, I realized that I was indeed starving. Luckily, this place started us out with bread baskets, just like the place where we had lunch.

The sun was getting low in the sky about the time we were finishing up with dinner. It caught my attention when it dropped low enough to shine through the restaurant windows and into my eyes. I glanced out the window and noticed a man standing next to our van. He seemed to be looking through the side windows near the back.

"What's that guy doing?" I asked. With the sun behind him it was hard to get a good look at him, but he was acting really nervous. I suppose I would be, too, if I was peeking into somebody's car. It looked like the same guy we had seen earlier.

We all just watched for a moment or two. Then, just as Dad started to get up from the table, the man turned away from our van, walked quickly across the parking lot, and disappeared. Dad hurried to the restaurant door and went outside. Brandon and I stood up to follow him, but Mom said, "Stay here, boys. Your father will handle whatever needs to be done."

"That looked like the same guy we saw at Isaac Morley's farm!" I said.

"I thought so too," said Brandon.

After a couple of minutes Dad came back inside. "I couldn't see where he went," he said. "He's gone."

CHAPTER 5

Marion, the Librarian

"If you want to call the FBI now," I said to Dad, "maybe it would be a good idea."

Dad looked surprised by my comment and said, "I'm sure it's nothing to worry about, Jeff." I just stared at him. Then Dad said, "A family with six children driving around in a huge van isn't nearly as common around here as it is in Utah. He's probably just a little curious."

I thought Dad was nuts, but I didn't say it out loud. No one else said anything either.

We were tired from a long day of driving, walking, and listening, so after finishing dinner, we just headed back to the hotel. Even with three full benches for the six of us to spread out on, we were irritable.

"Danny!" Chelsea said, "You're laying on my foot!"

"Well, your foot shouldn't be on the bench," Meg said.

"Well, he shouldn't be clear over here," Chelsea whined.

"Hey, guys," Dad cut in. "No quarreling, please. Chelsea, can you think of a nicer way to say what you need?"

Chelsea heaved a huge sigh, obviously wondering why she was the one Dad pointed out. She stared defiantly at Danny for a few moments and then an obvious change came over her face. She took a deep breath and said, "Danny, will you please move over to the other end of the bench?"

"Thanks, Chelsea," Dad said.

Danny sat up and said, "I would, but somebody put this big, blue book in my way."

"What?" Dad said, whipping his head around to see what Danny was talking about. The van swerved as he did it.

Mom gasped and grabbed the dashboard, but didn't say anything.

"Sorry," Dad said to her, returning his eyes to the road. "Is it *my* book?" he asked, now trying to see something through the rearview mirror. I was on the bench behind Danny and Chelsea, so I reached over and picked up the book. "It's yours, all right," I said.

"So that's where it was," said Mom.

"Was it there all along?" Dad asked.

"No!" Danny said, with a bit of disgust. "I was sitting there before, but now it's making me be too close to Chelsea and be on her foot."

"I don't think it was there before," said Shauna. "We looked everywhere back here."

"Was it there before we got to the restaurant?" asked Dad.

Nobody answered. "Danny!" Dad said. "Was the book there before we got to the restaurant?"

He just shrugged his shoulders, but didn't say anything. I figured Dad hadn't seen his gesture, so I said, "Danny says he doesn't know."

"Did we lock the van everywhere we went?" Dad asked Mom.

"Craig, I don't know," Mom said shaking her head back and forth. "That's *your* job."

We all knew what Mom meant.

"Dad," I said, "you lock everything, everywhere, every time. None of us ever even think about locking anything when you're around, because we know *you'll* do it!"

Dad thought for a moment before asking, "Do you lock anything when I'm *not* around?"

"Mom doesn't!" Brandon blurted out. Mom turned toward Dad with a big smile on her face and shrugged her shoulders. It was true. Mom locks practically nothing, anywhere, anytime.

"That's the way you guys are with everything!" Shauna said. "You don't do anything the same and you're both usually extreme on opposite ends!"

"We planned it that way when we got married," Dad said in a way that we knew he didn't expect anyone to believe it. "We did it so that each of you would have the full range of examples to choose from as you decide how you're going to live your lives." Now he was starting to sound a little sicky-sweet. "We just hope you choose something in the middle!"

"Your head is so full of . . ." Mom hesitated before continuing, "rules and laws and lists that I feel sorry for you. I know *I* wouldn't want to live in there." Turning toward the back of the van, she said to us, "Choose my way—it's a lot more fun!" She had a huge smile.

"Yeah!" Dad laughed. "Of course life is fun when you know that someone else is always locking all the doors for you!"

"Dad," Brandon said, "it's not that fun to go to 7–Eleven with you and then have to wait until you come out so I can get back in the car. Why do you lock it when we're only fifteen feet away?"

Dad started to defend himself, but decided to give it up. "Whatever," he mumbled. Then louder he asked, "So does anyone know for sure if the van was locked every time we got out of it today?"

No one did. Mom and Dad exchanged glances, but neither of them said anything. I thought about suggesting that Dad call the FBI again, but I didn't think he would, so I didn't bother.

"I'm sure I locked it every time," Dad said. "My binder must have been here all along."

• • •

54

Tuesday morning after eating breakfast in our hotel room, I asked, "Are we going to the library now?"

"No," Dad answered. "It doesn't open until ten."

"You're not going by your blue book again, are you?" Brandon asked.

Dad just smiled, refusing to be provoked. "No," he said slowly, "I saw a sign when we were there yesterday."

"How long will it take to get there?" Meg asked.

"Sixteen minutes," said Dad.

"Does that include U-turns?" I asked.

"There will be no U-turns necessary," Dad smiled. "We know how to get there."

"So what are we going to do?" Brandon asked.

"Family devotional," Dad said.

"Does it still count as a vacation if we have a devotional every day?" asked Brandon.

"It counts as a vacation *with a bonus!*" Dad smiled.

We sang "Families Can Be Together Forever" and then had a prayer.

"Let's start with a scripture in Malachi," Dad said. Then he had us all turn in our Bibles to the very last page of the Old Testament. Malachi 4:5–6 reads:

Behold, I will send you Elijah the prophet before the coming of the great and dreadful day of the Lord:

And he shall turn the heart of the fathers to the children, and the heart of the children to their fathers, lest I come and smite the earth with a curse.

"Your hearts are being turned to your fathers," Dad said.

"I noticed something a few years ago," Shauna said, "one time when our family did baptisms for the dead."

"What's that?" asked Mom.

"Well," Shauna continued, "I had always felt the Spirit when I did baptisms with the Young Women in our ward, but it felt completely different when we were doing it for our own relatives."

"How was it different?" Dad asked.

Shauna said, "I still felt good about doing the work, but it was just a lot more fun—and, I don't know, energizing—knowing that these people were part of my family."

"I know," I said. "I think about where they lived and the things they did and the decisions they made that put me where I am in the world and made our family what it is today."

"I wonder if Elias Franzen knows how much we know about him," Meg said. "And if he cares."

"I'm sure that he knows *and* he cares," said Dad.

We were all silent for a few moments. I think we were all just enjoying the Spirit. Then Meg asked, "Is that what it means when it says that the hearts of the fathers are turned to the children?"

Chelsea said to Dad, "I thought that meant just *you* taking care of *us*."

"I think that's part of it," Dad said. "But I think Meg is right, too. I think that when we do everything we can to help our ancestors through family history research and temple work, that they become free to help *us* and protect *us*."

Dad started turning pages in his Bible and said, "Do you remember the story of Elisha when they awoke one morning and found they were surrounded by men with horses and chariots and they thought they were about to be destroyed?"

We all stared blankly back at Dad, so he continued, "In 2 Kings, chapter six, at the end of verse fifteen we read, 'And his servant said unto him, Alas, my master! how shall we do?' He was afraid because he knew that they were seriously outnumbered. In verse sixteen we read what Elisha told him: 'Fear not: for they that be with us are more than they that be with them.' I imagine that the servant thought Elisha was crazy, because it was obvious to everyone on both sides that that wasn't true. But now listen to verse seventeen:

'And Elisha prayed, and said, Lord, I pray thee, open his eyes, that he may see. And the Lord opened the eyes of the young man; and he saw: and, behold, the mountain was full of horses and chariots of fire round about Elisha.'"

"Oh, yeah!" I said, "I remember this story from Sunday School."

"Me, too," said Brandon. "That's a cool story."

"I think the same is true for us," Mom said. "Just like Dad said: when we help our forefathers, they help us and protect us."

"Do you think Elias Franzen's forefathers helped him when he needed it?" asked Meg.

"I'm sure they did," Dad said.

"Can you tell us about them?" asked Meg.

"Nope," said Mom. Meg looked hurt. "We would if we could," Mom continued, "but so far Elias Franzen is the root of our family tree. We don't know who his parents are."

"Oh, sad!" whimpered Chelsea. "We need to find his parents." She was very sincere.

"We're working on it," Dad said. "But you're right—and it will be exciting when we find them, won't it? Remember how happy Lehi was when Nephi came back with the plates and he found his family history?"

"Oh, that's right!" said Shauna. "Lehi discovered that he was a descendant of Joseph."

We talked for a while about how important family history is and why we have all these temples. We also talked about how computers have made doing family history research so much easier and faster and how the Church now has so many more temples in the world where people can go to do the ordinances.

After the closing song and a family prayer, we all climbed into the van and headed for the Kirtland Public Library. As we drove, I found myself getting more and more excited about getting help from the librarian. When Dad parked the van, I immediately jumped out and was the first one inside the library.

"May I help you?" asked a man behind the desk who hadn't been there the day before.

"Hi," I said, as my family trailed in behind me. "We were told that a woman by the name of Marian would be working here today."

"If someone told you that, then they're a liar," said the man.

I didn't know what to say, so I just stammered for a moment. No one else seemed to know how to respond either. I think Dad was about to say something when the man said, "There's no *woman* here by that name. Only me. I'm Marion."

"Oh!" I said, my eyes wide. I felt really dumb. It made me wish that someone else had asked him instead of me. "I'm sorry, sir."

"Don't be sorry for me," the man said with a smile. "The other guy that works here is named Shirley. If you're going to be sorry for someone, be sorry for him. I've always reckoned I got the better end of the deal."

We all smiled at that.

"I reckon maybe you're right," Dad said. I thought it was funny how he liked to use the same words as people he was talking to. I never heard him say *reckon* when we were at home.

"Oh, I get it!" Meg giggled. "We never saw your name written down! If we had seen it, then we would have known—because the woman's name is spelled with an *a* and the man's name is spelled with an *o*."

"You're right!" smiled Marion.

I just stared at Meg in amazement. I was regularly surprised by the things that she knew. I figured it came from all the reading that she did.

"What can I do for you?" Marion asked.

"We were told that you can help us determine where the sun rises on a particular day of the year," Dad said.

"You want to know *where* the sun rises?" asked Marion. "Do you mean where on the horizon?"

"Yes," said Dad.

"And are we talking about here in Kirtland?" Marion asked.

"Right," Dad said.

Marion drew a deep breath. "It can be done," he said, "but it will take some work." He looked at us thoughtfully for a moment and then asked, "You folks from around here?"

"Actually, we're from Utah," Dad said. "We're just here on vacation."

Marion raised his eyebrows. Then he asked, "How'd you get my name?"

"We met a very nice couple who live just a few blocks from here," Mom explained.

"Rudy and Chloe?" Marion asked.

"That's right!" smiled Mom.

"They're the nicest folks I've ever known," said Marion. "Soon as you said 'very nice' I figured it had to be them."

We all just smiled.

"Well, let's see what we can find here," Marion said, turning to a computer terminal in front of him. He hit a few keys and waited for a moment, looking over the screen. Mumbling slightly to himself, he said, "Ohio," as he made a couple clicks with the mouse, then, "Kirtland," followed by another click. Looking up at Mom over the top of his glasses he asked, "Now what is the date you're interested in?"

"The shortest day of the year," Dad answered. After a pause, Dad asked, "Does it matter what year?"

Looking back down at the computer screen, Marion said, "Not for sunrise and sunset. It'll be essentially the same no matter what year you're talking about." He clicked a few more times and then said, "Now moonrise and moonset are a different matter."

Spinning the computer screen to where we could see it, Marion said, "Take a look here."

We all huddled in close as he pointed to things on the screen and continued to explain.

"This screen shows all the data for Kirtland, Ohio, on December twenty-first of this year." Marion looked up at Dad and said, "December twenty-first being the shortest day of the year."

"Right," said Dad, still looking at the screen.

Marion pointed to the screen and said, "As you can see here, the sunrise on that date is 7:49 A.M. Eastern Standard Time. Now you can see the times for everything else on that date, but you folks are just interested in the sunrise, correct?"

"That's right," Mom said.

"But now take a look at the time for moonrise," Marion said. "Looks like 5:47 A.M. Now let's change the date back to 1901— that's as far back as this will go—and take a look at the times."

Marion clicked the mouse a few times and then said, "Okay, now take a look at this." Pointing to the screen again he said, "See, the sunrise is the same: 7:49 A.M. But now take a look at the moon-rise—see where it says 1:57 P.M. there?"

"Oh, that's cool!" Brandon said.

"But now that's only half of what you need," Marion said, looking up. "We know the time of day, but I'll really need to do some digging to figure out where the sun is in its rotation at that time so that we can know where it is on the horizon." He leaned back in his chair and thoughtfully rubbed his chin a few times, staring up at the ceiling.

"So what exactly do you need this for?" Marion asked. "If you don't mind my asking."

"Not at all," said Mom. Turning to Dad, she asked, "Did you bring it in?"

I hadn't noticed before, but he was holding his blue binder. He opened it up to the last page where the old letter was now inside a plastic sheet protector.

"When did you put the letter in your binder?" I asked.

"This morning," Dad said.

"Impressive," said Marion as he looked the document over. Under his breath, he whispered, "July 1831."

"When we get back to Utah," Dad said, "we'll probably want to donate this to someone who can take better care of it."

I thought about the man who was missing with the *last thing* that we had donated. I wondered if Dad considered that to be taking "better care of it."

The other man, Shirley, came up to the desk and looked at the old letter in the notebook.

"So is this book full of other old documents like this?" Marion asked.

"No," smiled Dad. "That's the only one." With a look of pleasure at the thought of sharing his treasure with someone, Dad began flipping through the pages for Marion and Shirley to see. Dad said, "This is just information about where we're staying and places we're visiting and such."

As soon as Dad stopped talking and turning pages, Marion said, "What was it you were going to show me on that old document?"

Dad's smile faded a bit as he turned back to the letter. Shirley seemed disinterested and went off to do something else.

Mom said, "See this third paragraph here where it says '*the small hyding place that was markt and illuminated thru the attick window at dawn precisely on that day when the sun rises at its latest time all year.*' This letter was never delivered, and so we're thinking that this hiding place may still have something hidden in it."

"Do you really think you can figure out where the sun rises on December twenty-first?" I asked the librarian.

"I believe I can," Marion nodded. "But I reckon you won't be happy with the results."

Dad laughed and said, "Oh, don't worry. We hold only slim hope that something may still be there after all this time."

"That's good," said Marion. "But that's not what I mean."

"What do you mean then?" asked Mom.

"December twenty-first isn't the date you should be looking for," Marion explained.

"But *you* said that's the shortest day of the year," Brandon blurted out.

"Indeed it is," nodded Marion, "but the letter says the day when the sun rises at its *latest time*—not the shortest day."

We all just stared at him until he continued. "The sun continues to rise later and later for at least another two weeks," he said, "but because it sets so much later, the days are actually getting longer. So that means that the shortest day of the year is *not* the same as the day the sun rises at its latest time."

"Really?" asked Dad. "I had no idea."

Turning back to the computer screen, Marion nodded, "Yup. Let's take a look here." He brought up a calendar for the month of January and started looking at the dates. "Here we go," he said after a moment. "January tenth has the sun rising at 7:52 A.M." Leaning back in his chair and looking up at Mom and Dad again, he said, "Now three minutes and three weeks will make a significant difference."

"Really?" Dad said again. Marion nodded.

"So how long do you think it will take you to figure it out?" Brandon asked. Of course he was asking what we all wanted to know.

Marion rubbed his chin and said, "I'm going to need several days, I think."

"Days!" Brandon exclaimed.

I could see Dad elbow Brandon from where I was standing, but I think he did a good job of keeping it from where Marion could see it.

"That would be just fine," Dad said with a smile. "We appreciate how much time you've given us already. We're leaving town in a couple of days, but we'll be back next Tuesday."

Mom looked a little concerned. "It sounds like *way* too much work!" she said. "We can't ask you to do that!"

"Ah, now, don't worry about that," smiled Marion. "I don't think it will really take too much time, but I've got to gather a couple of resources first and I know that will take at least a couple of days. And besides, this is exactly the kind of thing that I enjoy doing." He looked sincere. "It will be a pleasure. And I'll do my best to have it ready by Tuesday."

"That will be great," Dad said. "Thanks."

We all thanked him and walked outside. Brandon let out a loud "Aarrgh!" that sounded exactly the way I felt. I couldn't believe we had to wait till Tuesday!

CHAPTER 6

The Family

That afternoon we went to some places that weren't Church history sites. During one family night, a couple of weeks before we left home, Mom and Dad had us look through some brochures about the places we were going to visit on this trip and let us each choose one place that we wanted to go. I said that I wanted to go to the Hard Rock Café and Brandon had said that he wanted to go to the Rock and Roll Hall of Fame, both of which were in downtown Cleveland. Dad didn't look too excited when we each announced what we wanted to do, but they were in the brochures, so Mom said it was great. (I noticed that she listens to rock music in the car a little more often that Dad does!) So the rest of the day became "Rock and Roll" day.

It was only about a fifteen minute drive from Kirtland to downtown Cleveland. The Rock and Roll Hall of Fame was right next to Lake Erie. It's called a lake, but it looks like an ocean, because it's huge! You can't see to the other side; it looks like it goes on forever. We took a walk by the lake for a few minutes before going inside the Hall of Fame. The place was at least five stories high, but for several hours we never made it off of the bottom floor—that's because that's where all the really old music was. Mom and Dad both really got into the music history section. They made us listen to all these people that were dead, probably before I was even born—and it didn't sound anything like rock and roll to me.

Supposedly, these were the people that had influenced the beginnings of rock and roll.

Shauna, Brandon, and I had moved ahead of the rest of the family and found this big wall of the biggest hits for each decade. We each put headphones on and were pushing buttons, listening to some of our favorite songs, when I felt someone tapping me on the shoulder. It was Dad. He had a huge, mischievous smile on his face. When Brandon and I took off our headphones he pointed to another display across the lobby from where we were. Shauna saw us and came over, too.

"Have you guys been over there?" Dad asked.

"No," we admitted. I had finally found something in this place I was enjoying, and I wasn't too hopeful that whatever he was talking about would be better than what we'd already found.

"What's the theme of our vacation this year?" Dad asked with a huge grin.

We all stuttered for a moment before Brandon said, "We have a—*theme?*"

Dad couldn't wait for us to get the right answer, so he just blurted out, "Family history! Genealogy! Knowing our lineage!"

We just stared at him, having no clue what he might have found.

"You know what a pedigree chart is, right?" Dad asked, still with enthusiasm.

"Is that the one with the . . . the . . . ," I began. I always got all those charts mixed up.

"That's the one that looks like branches of a tree going sideways," Dad said. "It starts with one person and then shows the two parents of that person, and then it shows the two parents of those two and so on and so on. Remember?"

"Oh, yeah," Brandon and I mumbled. I caught myself glancing back at the greatest hits wall, wondering if I was ever going to get to listen to anything else over there.

Dad looked at us with satisfaction and said with a smug look, "Every song has a pedigree."

"Wait, what?" Shauna said. It was the first noise she had made since Dad had interrupted our greatest hits experience.

"Every song has a pedigree," Dad said again. "Other songs that came before it and influenced its sound or rhythm or whatever else." He was getting way excited. "Come here!" he said as he started across the lobby. "This is really cool! I think you'll like it."

I must admit, he was right: it *was* really cool. There were booths where several people could stand at once. On the wall was a screen that you could touch to select different songs on the "pedigree chart." Part of the song would play when you selected it. But the cool part was selecting the "parents" on the pedigree chart. You really could hear how the sound and style of the older song was used when the new song was created. And the pedigree charts expanded into all different styles and types of music. Shauna, Brandon, and I must have hung out in that booth for close to an hour. We checked out practically every line on the pedigree chart. Personally, I thought it was a stretch to claim that this display somehow made the Rock and Roll Hall of Fame part of the "theme" of our family vacation, but I figured if it made Dad feel better, why not go with it? When we finally did make our way back to the greatest hits display, I asked Shauna, "Since when do we have a theme for family vacations?" She just shrugged her shoulders and put on some headphones.

Sometime later Mom and Dad found us again and asked if we were hungry. We found a café on one of the upper levels and sat down at two small round tables that we pushed together, making a table in the shape of a figure eight. I guess they didn't have too many huge families eat together at the Rock and Roll Hall of Fame. Probably because the price of a simple hamburger was roughly equivalent to the price of a classic album.

As we ate, we started talking about the things we had seen. After a few minutes Dad brought up the pedigree charts again.

"It's interesting to see how much everything is influenced by what's around us," Dad said. "Just like musicians are influenced by other musicians, people in general are influenced by friends and family."

Mom said, "I wonder how many of those families living on Isaac Morley's farm would have joined the Church if they hadn't all been living together."

"Because of their influence on each other?" Dad asked.

"Yes," Mom nodded.

"So did Elias Franzen live on Isaac Morley's farm with everybody else?" Brandon asked. "Did he give them all his money and stuff, too—so that everyone could share it?"

"Is that why he joined the Church?" Meg asked.

"I don't think so," Mom said. "I think he just knew what was going on and then joined the Church about the same time as they did."

"How do you know that?" asked Meg.

"Just from things we've found while doing our family history work," Mom said. For the next few minutes Mom and Dad told us tons of things they knew about Elias Franzen. He was still a young man at the time all of this was going on. He got to know Joseph Smith pretty well in the first few months after the Prophet first moved to Kirtland. It was fun to think about having a triple great-grandfather who did all the cool stuff that he did.

"Do you know things about other people we're related to?" Meg asked.

"Of course," said Mom. "Would you like to hear about some of them sometime?"

Danny and Chelsea made the most noise, saying, "Yeah!" but I think we all felt pretty much the same.

"Do you think that Elias's friend—whatever his name was—Blaine something—lived on Isaac Morley's farm?" Brandon asked.

"Wright," Dad said.

"You mean 'right,' he *did* live on the farm?" asked Brandon.

"No, *Wright*," said Dad. "His name was Blaine *Wright*."

"Oh," grunted Brandon. "So did he live on the farm or not?"

"I don't know," Dad confessed. "All we know about him is from that letter."

Shauna's mouth fell open and she gave a huge gasp. "Do you know what *I* think?" We all just stared at her. "I think he was *going* to join them."

"Really?" Dad said.

"Didn't the letter say something about him wanting to join himself to 'The Family' or something like that?" Shauna asked.

"Oh, yeah," I said. "And that's what they called themselves, isn't it? Isn't that what the missionaries at Isaac Morley's farm said?"

"I think you may be right," Mom said. "When we get back to the car we can check it out for sure."

Brandon was horrified. "You *left* it in the car! The letter? What if it gets stolen?"

Mom looked like she couldn't believe he was serious. Slowly she said, "I'm sure Dad locked it." Looking at Dad, she smiled and added, "He always does."

"I made sure it was locked," Dad agreed. "The letter is inside my blue binder."

"The one that already got stolen once and then returned to the van?" I asked. I had to agree with Brandon on this one.

"We don't know for sure that it was taken and then put back," Mom said. Dad looked at her like *he* knew for sure, even if she didn't.

"I think we should keep it in Meg's backpack," Brandon said. "She *always* has it on." Turning to Meg, another look of shock came over his face and he said, "Where is it?"

"We had to check it at the coatroom," Dad smiled. "They don't let people bring anything like that in here."

"Well, even *that* would be a lot safer than in the van," Brandon said. "We should go get it and put it in Meg's backpack in the coatroom *right now!*"

Dad screwed up his face a little and then, after a pause, said, "I don't think we need to do that." Another pause. "I *really* don't want to do that."

"I'm sure it will be fine," Mom agreed. "We can look at the letter when we're done here."

Brandon slumped back into his chair like he couldn't believe how reckless our parents were.

"When we go out," Meg smiled, "you can put it in my backpack if you want."

"Thanks, Meg," Dad said. "That'll be great."

The rest of the afternoon, Brandon acted like he was having a terrible time. Every twenty minutes or so he would ask, "Should we go now?" or something like that. After a while, Mom and Dad didn't even bother to answer him. They weren't done and they weren't in a hurry, either.

When we finally left the building late in the afternoon, Brandon took Dad's keys and ran ahead to check on the letter in the van.

"Will you go with Brandon, please?" Dad said to me.

I was slightly annoyed by the request. I wasn't the one who was worried about the letter, and I really had no interest in running all the way to the van just so Brandon could finally chill about it. But I knew from experience that it really wasn't worth arguing about—apparently, Dad thought the Cub Scout buddy system was a lifelong requirement. So I followed Brandon without bothering to complain. But I didn't bother to go near as fast as Brandon, either. I figured as long as I kept him in sight, that made me a good enough "buddy."

I wasn't sure which would have made Brandon happier:

discovering that the letter was safe, or proving to everyone in the family that he was right to be worried, because the letter had indeed been stolen. It turns out, though, that everything was fine. The book was right where Dad had left it, and the letter was safely inside the book.

When everyone else got back to the van, pretty much everyone wanted to read the letter because we had just been talking about it. Shauna read it out loud for us as we all sat in the van in the parking lot.

"Oh, yeah," I said. "I'd forgotten that part about The Family getting disbanded. I remember thinking, *How does a family get disbanded?* but I never remembered to ask."

"What does *disbanded* mean?" Chelsea asked.

"It means that it was taken apart," said Dad, "or that it wasn't together anymore."

"That doesn't really make sense for a real family," Mom said, "but it sure sounds like what happened to The Family group at Isaac Morley's farm."

"Do you think that's what Elias was talking about in the letter?" I asked.

"It sure makes sense," Dad agreed. "It sounds like Blaine Wright went to Pennsylvania to sell his farm so that he could donate the money to Isaac Morley's group."

Shauna said, "But when he got back they had all joined the Church, right?"

"That's what it sounds like," said Dad.

Brandon asked, "What's the scripture that the people on Isaac Morley's farm were going by when they decided to live together and share everything?"

"Good question," said Dad. "We can look it up when we get back to the hotel room."

"Aren't we going to the Hard Rock Café now?" I asked.

"I have my little scriptures in my backpack," Meg said.

"Oh!" Mom smiled. "You're such a good girl, Meg. But I think it would be nice if we all had our scriptures when we look it up. And besides that, aren't you hungry?"

"Starved!" agreed Meg.

"Let's go to the Hard Rock Café!" said Dad.

As we drove out of the parking lot, Dad said to Brandon, "Thanks for choosing the Hall of Fame, Brandon. That was fun."

"I thought it was fun, too," Brandon said, "Thanks for taking us." I figured now that he knew the letter was safe, he was able to enjoy the *memory* of the Hall of Fame, even if he had made himself miserable all afternoon.

"When are we going to do *my* choice?" asked Danny.

"Have you decided what you want to do yet?" Mom asked.

"No," said Danny flatly.

Mom smiled. "We'll decide *when* we're going to do your choice as soon as we know what your choice is, okay?"

"Okay," Danny said glumly.

We had a great time at dinner—the food was really good. Mom and Dad had fun looking at the stuff all over the walls. Most of the music that was playing while we were there was older stuff that Mom and Dad liked, but I had never heard before. There were a few songs that I knew, though.

As we walked out Dad said, "Thanks for choosing the Hard Rock Café, Jeff. That was good!"

"You're welcome," I said. "Thanks for taking us."

Danny asked, "When are you going to do *my* choice?"

Mom asked him, "Have you decided what it is yet?"

"Oh, yeah," said Danny. "Never mind."

When we got back to the hotel, Dad had us look up *United Order* in the Topical Guide. All it said was "*see* Consecration," so we went there. The very first scripture listed is Acts 2:44 which reads:

And all that believed were together, and had all things common.

"That's what The Family was doing, right?" Brandon asked.

"Right," said Dad, "but take a look at verse forty-five." He read it aloud for us. "And sold their possessions and goods, and parted them to all men, as every man had need."

"*That's* what that Blaine Wright guy was doing, isn't it?" said Shauna. "He went to Pennsylvania to sell his farm so he could join The Family and give them the money."

"I think you're right," said Mom. "There's another scripture listed that talks about it some more." She read Acts 4:32–37 for us. It says that people didn't claim anything that they had as their own. They sold whatever they had and brought it to the Apostles so that they could give it to those who needed it.

"But the people living on Isaac Morley's farm stopped doing that when they joined the Church, right?" Shauna asked.

"That's right," said Dad.

"Do you remember that people in the Book of Mormon lived like that too for a while?" Mom asked.

"Really?" I said.

"After Christ appeared in America," Mom continued, "the people had all things in common for almost two hundred years."

We didn't find anything else listed in the Topical Guide, so Dad suggested that we look in the Book of Mormon index. Under the word *Common* we found a couple of references about it. In 3 Nephi 26:19 we read: *And they taught, and did minister one to another; and they had all things common among them, every man dealing justly, one with another.*

In 4 Nephi 1:3 it states: *And they had all things common among them; therefore there were not rich and poor, bond and free, but they were all made free, and partakers of the heavenly gift.*

In verses 24 and 25 of that same chapter we read that about two hundred years after the birth of Christ, some of the people started wearing "fine things of the world" and so after that, they stopped having things in common.

We talked for a while about what it might be like to try to live that way. Dad gave us some examples of how it might be if we tried it just in our own family. It didn't seem like such a great idea to me. I just couldn't understand how it would be to give everything away and let someone else decide what I needed and what I didn't. I was amazed that the Book of Mormon people were able to do it as long as they did.

Wednesday we spent the whole day in downtown Cleveland again. We got there in time for an early lunch from a street vendor and then went to the Children's Science Museum. That was what Chelsea had chosen for her family vacation activity. Mom and Dad love to take us to science museums wherever we go. My favorite one had always been the one in Las Vegas. I thought Chelsea was silly to make the museum her choice, though, because I figured there was a pretty good chance Mom and Dad would drag us there anyway.

We spent a very long afternoon at the science museum. When I say "long," I don't mean that I didn't like it; it was actually pretty great. In fact, I liked this one even more than the one in Las Vegas. It was quite a bit bigger and had some really cool things that I'd never seen before. One of my favorites was playing soccer goal-keeper with a blue screen background while watching soccer balls flying toward us on a big-screen TV. When we were done we could watch ourselves on instant replay. The other thing that was really fun was the hang glider. It was a real hang glider that you could strap yourself into and when you moved the bar, the video display in front of you would change as if you were really flying. I had a great time and flew for several minutes above and through all these canyons that looked a lot like southern Utah. Brandon did it too, but he got bored after about half a minute and flew himself straight into the side of a huge cliff.

On the way out of the science museum we walked past a huge display of satellite TV monitors and saw that one of them was BYU-TV—and our stake president from Orem was on! We changed the display so we could hear what he was saying. We found that he was part of a discussion about the Book of Mormon. It was amazing to find that he was talking about the importance of records and the reasons that Nephi went back to get the brass plates. One of the reasons he mentioned was that the plates contained Lehi's family history. That made us all smile.

As we were climbing into the van, Mom said, "That science museum was my favorite one yet. Thanks, Chelsea."

"You're welcome!" Chelsea beamed.

Danny started to say, "When are we going to . . . ," but he stopped short and then quietly said, "Never mind." We all tried not to laugh.

"Do you need some help with ideas?" Shauna asked.

"No," Danny mumbled.

Thursday morning after breakfast we had to pack everything so that we could check out. This part of our vacation was going to be the longest drive of the trip. Dad said it would take four or five hours to get to Rochester, New York, where we would be staying. We were going there to visit Church history sites around Palmyra. We were also going to see the Hill Cumorah Pageant. But the first thing we were going to see in Rochester was the Memorial Art Gallery. This was Shauna's choice for the trip. She had been way into art ever since she took her first art appreciation class at BYU. Dad, the guy who liked saving a buck whenever he could, discovered that on Thursday evenings from 5–9 we could all get in for less than half the regular price, so—obviously—that's what he was going for. So, after checking the "estimated time" in his big blue binder, he decided that he wanted to leave for Rochester no later than 11:00 A.M. We came pretty close.

I slept most of the time in the van. I had been looking forward to maybe watching a couple of movies on Shauna's borrowed computer, but the girls all wanted to watch *Pride and Prejudice*.

"How long is it?" Brandon asked.

"I'm not sure," said Shauna, looking at the double-wide DVD case. "Oh, it looks like there are six one-hour episodes!"

"Six hours?" said Brandon. "You're not going to watch every one of them right now are you?"

"No, we won't have time," Meg smiled. "But we're going to have a marathon, huh, Shauna?"

"That's the plan," said Shauna. Then to Brandon and me Shauna said, "Have you guys ever seen it? It's really good."

Brandon and I both just sort of mumbled our response. Shauna was on the middle bench with Meg and Chelsea where they could all see the screen on Shauna's lap pretty easily. Brandon and I were on the bench behind, so it took a little more effort to watch—it wasn't worth it. I sort of listened to it for a while, but soon fell asleep.

Even though we were going to be getting into the art gallery for less than half price, Dad wanted to get his money's worth. We got into Rochester about 4:00 P.M. and found our hotel—but Dad didn't want to go in yet. He just wanted to know where it was. Instead, we went out to dinner and then straight to the art gallery. We were standing at the ticket window ten minutes early, waiting for the magic, cheapo 5 o'clock hour to arrive. The ticket lady got tired of watching us wait and let us in a few minutes early for the reduced price. They actually had some pretty cool stuff there. The paintings were okay, I guess, but my favorite part was the display of Egyptian coffins. It was amazing what these people did in honor of their dead ancestors. It made me think about how much we do or don't do for ours.

When the museum kicked us out at 9:00 P.M., we finally headed for our hotel. All the kids waited in the van while Mom and Dad went inside the hotel to register. They had told us that we were going to have a two-bedroom suite at this place just like the last one, since it was the same hotel chain. Ten minutes later Mom and Dad opened their doors and climbed back inside.

"I didn't give our itinerary to anyone," Dad said to Mom. "Did you?"

"No," Mom said. "I told the neighbors basically where we were going, but certainly not which hotel or any details like that."

"But we're talking about someone who's *here*," said Dad, "not at home."

They just stared at each other like they were trying to figure something out.

"What's going on?" Shauna asked in a groggy voice. She must have fallen asleep between the art gallery and the hotel.

"Well," Dad said after a heavy sigh. "We're all checked in; everything is fine." He paused before saying, "But as we were leaving the front desk, the manager walked by and glanced at our reservation on the computer screen." Dad looked over at Mom.

Mom continued where Dad left off by saying, "And then she said something like, 'Oh, *you're* the Andrews family? It's nice to have you with us. Someone came in earlier asking if you had arrived yet.'"

CHAPTER 7

Palmyra

"Who was it?" asked Chelsea.

"That's what we were just trying to figure out," said Dad.

"Did anyone know that we were going to be staying here?" asked Shauna.

"No," Mom answered. "That's what we were just discussing."

"I didn't give an itinerary to anyone," Dad said. "And the only place I have it written down is in my blue binder."

Brandon gasped. "Dad!" he breathed. "That's why someone took it that day! So they could find out where we were going to be next!"

Dad didn't look convinced. "I still think the book was probably in the van the whole time," he said.

Brandon got a look on his face that matched what I was thinking: *Are you serious?*

"But how else would someone know?" Meg asked.

Mom and Dad couldn't come up with anything, but they just didn't believe the missing notebook had anything to do with it.

"The notebook can't just magically reappear," said Brandon.

"In a family like this," Mom said, "you'd be surprised how often that's *exactly* how it seems."

The layout of this two-bedroom suite was different from the last one, but the sleeping arrangements were just the same. After driving most of the day and spending the entire evening at the art gallery, we were all too tired to do much else. So after we loaded up the refrigerator and kitchen cupboards with the food that we had left over from our room in Ohio, we all watched a movie together on TV. It was about a family that adopts a mouse and treats him like one of the kids. It was a crazy movie, but at least for me it helped take my mind off of the weird thing about someone asking for us at the front desk.

Friday morning Dad let us sleep in again. I decided that was the best part about this vacation. During the school year we never got to sleep in—even on weekends. Dad still got us up for family devotional every morning. And in the summer when he worked, he would get us up for devotional before he left. At least he did it later than on school days.

Friday afternoon it was time to do Meg's family activity. She had wanted all of us to check out books from a library, but since public libraries generally check out books only to people who live there, she agreed that going to a bookstore and buying a book would be even better. That way she would get to keep the book forever. Mom thought it was a pretty good idea, too. She saw this as an opportunity for our family to get some new books without incurring any overdue fines.

Of course we had to find a "good" bookstore. That took a couple of hours to accomplish, and then once we found this "good" bookstore, we had to browse for what seemed like another couple of hours. We did find some pretty great books on sale, though, so I think we all came away pretty happy with the whole event.

As we climbed back into the van, Dad said, "Thanks, Meg. That was fun."

"Good choice," Mom agreed.

I waited to see if Danny was going to say anything, but he didn't. It looked like he was sure thinking about it though. And by the time we got to our hotel and were climbing out of the van, he had apparently made his decision.

"When are we going to do what *I* want?" Danny said.

"Have you decided *what* you want yet?" Mom asked.

"Yes," said Danny, forcefully. At this news, the entire family erupted into a cheer.

"How long are we going to be staying in *this* place?" Danny asked.

"Three more nights," replied Dad.

"Are we going to be at this hotel place part of the time, too?" asked Danny.

"Yes," Dad said.

"Does this hotel have a swimming pool like our last place?"

"It does," Mom said.

"Because," said Danny emphatically, "we were at the last place for lots of days and I never got to do the thing that *I* wanted to do— and that's to go swimming with our whole family."

"That's because you never told us that's what you wanted!" Dad smiled.

"That's because I didn't know yet!" said Danny. Everyone laughed.

"I'm glad you've decided, now, Daniel," Mom said.

"Can we all go swimming now?" asked Danny.

"Not tonight," said Dad. "The pool is outside, so we'll want to go during the day."

"Can we do it very first—tomorrow morning?" Danny asked.

"You can," Mom smiled, "and the rest of the kids can go with you. But Dad and I are going to the temple. We can all swim together when Dad and I get back."

"Oh, fun!" said Shauna. "I forgot they have a temple here now."

"It's great, isn't it?" said Dad.

"If you go really early," I said, "then we can all go swimming when you get back."

"That would work at home," Mom said, "but this is a smaller temple, so they only do sessions at certain times on certain days."

"In fact," said Dad, "I called ahead weeks ago to make

reservations. And by the time I called, there was only one session left that had room for us."

"You don't have to make reservations when we're at home, do you?" I asked.

"No," Mom said. "The bigger temples have sessions pretty much all day every day."

"Are you going to be doing it for our ancestors?" Meg asked.

"Yep," Dad nodded. "We brought some family cards with us."

"Are their hearts going to be turned to us?" Meg asked.

"We hope so!" answered Mom.

"It seems funny to me," I said, "that the scripture about turning the hearts of fathers to children and children to fathers is in the Old Testament, but now it's like what—two thousand years later—that we *finally* have the temples to do all the work."

"Jesus was born two thousand years ago," Shauna said, "and didn't Malachi—the prophet who said that—live a few hundred years before that?"

"That's right," Dad nodded to Shauna. Then turning back to me he said, "But if you look, I think you'll find scriptures about turning hearts between fathers and children in the New Testament, and the Book of Mormon, and the Doctrine and Covenants as well." He thought for a moment and then said, "You'll even find something in the Pearl of Great Price."

"Really?" Brandon said.

"Why don't you see if you can find them?" Mom suggested.

We all just stared at each other. Then Dad got a mischievous smile on his face and said, "Tell you what: the first person who finds a scripture reference about turning the hearts of the fathers to the children and the hearts of the children to the fathers in *all five* books of scripture—gets to choose where we go to dinner."

"I'm *there!*" yelled Brandon as he ran to get his scriptures. I was right behind him. "We haven't had pizza for*ever*," Brandon said as he hurried back to the kitchen table where Shauna was sitting, "and that's what I'm choosing!"

Shauna groaned at the word *pizza* and immediately jumped up from the kitchen table to get her scriptures. "*I'm* going to win," she said firmly, "if only to keep us from having pizza! Again!"

"What do mean *again?*" asked Brandon. "It's been *days*—almost a *week!*"

"I have a question," said Meg. She was standing in the middle of the family room holding her scriptures. "I thought we only had *four* books of scripture." Turning to Dad she asked, "Didn't you say we had to find it in all *five* books?"

"I counted the New Testament separately from the Old Testament," Dad smiled.

"Oh-h-h!" Meg giggled. "I get it." She plopped down on the floor where she had been standing and immediately began flipping through pages.

"This is going to take forever," Chelsea said with a sigh.

"I know," said Danny. "I would try, but I can't read all those books very fast."

Dad laughed. "You don't have to read all the books, remember? That's why we have a Topical Guide."

"Oh, yeah," said Chelsea without enthusiasm. "But still—we have to find *five* different ones."

"Bring me your scriptures," said Dad. "I'll show you how to do it."

As Chelsea went to get her scriptures, Dad said, "You just have to pick a big word that's part of the scripture about turning the hearts of the fathers and the children and find it in the Topical Guide. Then you find the listing that we already know about in Malachi and look for any other scriptures listed right there with it."

"That's what I did!" called Brandon. "And I found a reference in the Book of Mormon! But's that's the only one."

"What is it?" asked Mom. Dad was now busy helping Chelsea and Danny find the Topical Guide.

"Third Nephi 25:6," said Brandon.

"What word did you look up?" asked Dad.

"*Curse!*" said Brandon. "I've always liked scriptures that have cursing in them!"

Mom sort of laughed, but Dad's jaw just dropped open as he looked up from Chelsea's book and stared at Brandon.

"Don't worry, Dad," said Brandon with slight disgust, "that's as close as I get to it."

"I've got all the other books," said Shauna.

"Me, too!" I called.

"Did you two look up the same word?" asked Dad.

"I used *children*," said Shauna.

"Mine is *heart*," I said.

"What's a reference in the New Testament?" asked Mom.

At the same time, Shauna and I both said, "Luke 1:17!"

"Good job!" Mom said. "How about the Doctrine and Covenants?"

Again Shauna and I spoke at the same time. I said, "Doctrine and Covenants 2:2," while Shauna said, "Doctrine and Covenants 2:1–3."

"That sounds like pretty much the same one," Mom smiled.

"And I'm glad to hear you both saying *Doctrine and Covenants*," Dad interjected, "and not *D&C!*"

(Anytime someone in our family says *D&C*, Dad always says, "That's just the abbreviation. That's not the way we should say it!" Then he would give some example—a different one almost every time—that went something like, "We don't say *Matt* when we're talking about the *Gospel of Matthew*," or "We don't say *Hela* when we're talking about the *Book of Helaman*." Personally, my favorite example was, "We don't say *Rev* when we're talking about the *Revelation of St. John the Divine*." The word *Rev* made me think of a nickname for a reverend. Sometimes I would say *D&C* on purpose, just hoping that Dad would use the "Rev" example again when he told me not to say the abbreviation.)

This time, though, we all pretty much ignored Dad's comment about *D&C*. We had more important things on our mind.

"How about a reference in the Pearl of Great Price," Mom said.

"JS–H is in the Pearl of Great Price, isn't it?" I asked. "Isn't that the abbreviation for Joseph Smith—History?" I looked over at Dad as I said the word *abbreviation*, wondering if he would notice. He didn't.

"Yeah, it is," Shauna said in answer to my question. "Is your reference chapter 1, verse 39?"

"Yep!" I said. Then I added, "Wahoo! Shauna and I win. We got the rest of them. How do we split who gets to choose dinner?"

"You would need to split with Brandon, too," said Mom. "You couldn't have done it without him." That comment stopped me cold in the middle of my victory celebration.

"I could have," said Meg. We all turned to look at her. "I found Luke 1:17, 3 Nephi 25:6, Doctrine and Covenants 27:9, and two more in the Doctrine and Covenants, and Joseph Smith—History 1:39."

"Great work!" said Dad. "What was your word?"

"*Turn*," said Meg.

"*Turn?*" I asked in disbelief. "What made you think to use the word *turn?*"

"Because," Meg said, "I think that's the most important word in the scripture. I always think of it like we're looking the other way. And until we actually *turn* to look at our ancestors, we won't ever see them or think about them or help them."

The silence in the room after that comment was amazing. She was right. And the Spirit in the room after she said it was a testimony to each of us of the importance of actually turning ourselves toward our forefathers and doing all that we can to bless them.

"Well done," Mom said quietly. There was another pause. "I think you win."

Dad nodded. "I agree," he said. "Where would you like to eat, Meg?"

Brandon got a look on his face that clearly said he thought he might still have a chance of getting what he wanted. "What do you like on your *pizza*, Meg?" Brandon asked slowly.

She looked over at him like she wasn't sure what he was trying to say.

"Where's your favorite place to *get* pizza, Meg?" Brandon continued.

Her eyelids fluttered just a bit as she considered this for a moment. Before she said anything, Brandon said, "Do you like places that have breadsticks and dipping sauce?" he asked.

"That's enough," Dad said finally.

"But she might *want* pizza," Brandon defended himself.

"If she does," Mom said, "then she can decide that without any *lobbying* from you. Just leave the campaign posters at home, okay?"

Brandon just got a big grin on his face. He obviously thought it was at least worth a try.

• • •

Saturday morning Mom and Dad left about 8:30 for the temple. We had breakfast together in the lobby and then came back to our room for a family prayer before they left. They were no sooner out the door when Danny said, "Can we go swimming now? Mom and Dad said we could while they were gone!"

I don't think any of us were too excited by the idea—except for Chelsea, that is. But Shauna was willing to go just for Danny, and she talked the rest of us into it as well. Normally we all like swimming, just not at 8:30 in the morning.

We all crammed together as we waited for Shauna to figure out which way to insert our room access card to let us through the gate into the pool area.

"How come you like swimming so much?" I asked Danny.

"I don't know," he shrugged. "I've just *always* really liked water a *lot.*"

"Not always," Brandon laughed.

"Uh-huh!" Danny whined.

Shauna finally got the gate open, and we followed her through onto the pool deck.

"Jeff," Brandon said to me, "remember the time we went on that ride that got us all wet and Danny was *so* mad!"

"Ha!" I laughed. "Yeah. That was so funny!"

"Was that the place where he got really mad and then made us take him on it again the next day?" Meg asked.

Almost at the same time Brandon and I said, "It made me mad! Two times!" Then all of us started laughing.

"Okay!" Danny pouted with his lips scrunched together. "I guess I didn't *always* like water a lot, so maybe I just liked it a little before."

We continued to laugh as we jumped into the warm water and began splashing around. Chelsea had brought some pool toys from home that she liked throwing into the middle part of the pool. She and Danny would jump in after them and try to bring them up as fast as they could. We must have been out there for at least a couple of hours. We had races and played some games.

We were in the middle of a game of Marco Polo when Brandon hissed, "*Jeff!*" from halfway across the pool.

"Brandon," Meg sang with her eyes squished tightly together, "I can hear you!" Meg was "it" and so the rest of us were only supposed to be saying "Polo" whenever she said "Marco."

"Quick, look at that guy!" Brandon hissed again, pointing toward a door that led from the parking lot into the lobby of the hotel. I looked up just in time to see a man with long, brown hair, a beard, and a yellow straw hat going into the building.

"Is that the same guy?" Shauna asked in total disbelief.

"It looked like it to me!" Brandon said.

"How did he get *here?*" Shauna asked.

None of us had an answer for that.

"Is the room locked?" Brandon asked. He acted a little frantic. "I think that's where the letter is. Or did Dad take his notebook with him?"

Nobody knew for sure. We hadn't really looked too closely at them as they left.

"He had it in the room this morning," Shauna said, "but I have no idea if he took it with him or not."

"Is the room locked?" Brandon asked again.

"It's always locked," Shauna answered. "As long as the door gets closed all the way."

"Who was the last one out?" I asked.

We couldn't decide, but it seemed like we all remembered hearing a pretty good-sized click as we left the room.

"Why don't we just all go back to the room now," Shauna suggested, climbing out of the pool. "We've already been here a long time."

Danny complained a bit, but we promised him that we would come back after Mom and Dad got home. The door leading to our room was on the opposite side of the pool area from where the man had gone inside toward the lobby, so we all just grabbed our stuff and ran inside.

As we were making our way down the hall, Brandon stopped short and said, "Jeff, come with me for a minute."

Shauna said, "Guys, don't do anything dumb."

Brandon looked like he couldn't believe she could even think such a thing. "Of *course* we won't," he said.

"Don't go near that guy," Shauna warned.

"We won't," Brandon said. "I promise."

"I know *I* won't," I said, shaking my head back and forth. I could feel my eyes bulging out a bit.

"Then where are you going?" Shauna asked.

"No time to explain," Brandon called over his shoulder as he ran down the hall back the way we had come.

Shauna looked slightly annoyed. "Go with him, Jeff!" she said to me. "And don't let him do anything stupid!"

"I'll try!" I called back to her as I ran after Brandon. "But I can't always stop him!"

I heard the door slam shut after Shauna and the little guys went into our room. I found myself wondering if we should have all just stayed together.

Brandon went down to the end of the building and outside through a different door that led directly to the parking lot.

"What are we doing?" I hissed, looking around for any sign of the long-haired man.

"Help me check for cars with Ohio license plates," Brandon panted, as he scurried into the parking lot. I'm sure we both looked pretty funny in our swimsuits with towels around our shoulders and water still dripping from our ears and noses.

I kept a close watch on the doors into the hotel as we scanned the parking lot. We found three cars with Ohio license plates.

"This is the one," Brandon said matter-of-factly.

"How do you know?" I asked.

"Because it *looks* like a crook's car!" Brandon said.

"What does *that* mean?" I asked.

"It's old and beat up!" Brandon said. "Crooks are crooks because they don't have enough money and so they steal things and become crooks!"

"*What* are you *talking* about?" I asked. "*Rich* people can be crooks, too, you know. That's how they got rich!"

"Well," Brandon said, pretty much ignoring my logic. "I just think it's this one."

There wasn't much to say in response to reasoning like that, so I just wandered slowly over to one of the other cars with Ohio license plates. I walked around it a couple of times and then—after checking the doors into the building once more—I started looking inside the windows to see what I might find.

"I think it's *this* one," I called over to Brandon after a minute.

"Why?" he asked, sounding pretty much uninterested.

I called back, "Because there's a copy of Elias Franzen's document sitting on the front seat!"

CHAPTER 8

Hill Cumorah Pageant

"What?" yelled Brandon. "No way!" He was running toward me as he yelled. "Where?" he breathed as he stooped over next to the car window.

"Right there," I said, pointing.

Brandon stared through the window at the paper on the passenger seat. "No way!" he hissed. He paused, panted several times and then said, "No way!" again. He stared at the paper for several more moments and then suddenly jerked his head up and looked at each of the hotel doors in turn.

"Who *is* that guy?" Brandon panted. "And how did he get that?"

"I don't know," I said, watching the doors.

"I bet it's the guy from the archives," said Brandon. "The one that's missing!"

"Why do you think that?" I asked. "It's not the *original* document. It's just a copy!"

"Well if the guy has the *original*," Brandon said with irritation in his voice, "then he *certainly* could make a copy of it, couldn't he?"

I just stared at him.

"And besides that," Brandon said, "on the *copy* you can read the words that he told to Meg."

This comment made me immediately pull my eyes away from the hotel doors and look at the paper through the window once again. I hadn't noticed it before, but Brandon was right: the note was clearly visible along the edge of the page. I read the words half out loud: *Dear Hannah, Carry on efforts to assure that B. Wright retrieved his funds from my Kirtland home. Love, -D.*

"Is that the way that Meg had it written?" I asked.

"Sounds close enough," Brandon said. "It's *got* to be the Granite Guy!"

"Granite Guy?" I questioned.

"Yeah," Brandon nodded. "The archives are kept inside that granite vault, remember?"

"Oh," I mumbled. Then I said, "But remember that Dad said the FBI agent acted like he already had a copy of the message, too. Maybe it's him with a fake beard and wig."

"Agent Tassle-Shoes?" Brandon asked. "Why would he dress up funny and follow us?"

"Why would *anybody* dress up funny and follow us?" I asked. My eyes were back on the doors.

"What makes you think that guy's hair and beard are fake?" Brandon asked. "If they were fake, he wouldn't keep wearing the same thing every place he follows us to, would he?"

"How would *I* know?" I asked. "*You're* the one who can read criminal minds!"

"Whatever," Brandon mumbled.

"We better go back to the room," I suggested.

"What?" Brandon glared at me. "Why?"

"To make sure everybody is okay!" I said.

"No way," Brandon said, shaking his head. "I'm not letting this car out of my sight!"

"So what are you going to do if the guy comes back out?" I asked in disbelief.

"I don't know," Brandon mumbled. "Something, though."

"You're nuts," I said.

Just then I heard something that was almost too much to hope for at that moment: the sound of Mom and Dad's van turning into the hotel parking lot. I didn't realize how uptight I had been feeling until seeing that van made my whole body relax. I heard myself let out a huge sigh. As they drove closer to where we were, Brandon started jumping up and down and waving his hands all over the place. It was kind of embarrassing.

"Brandon!" I hissed. "I'm sure they see us."

"I want to be sure," Brandon said between jumps.

As Dad pulled into a parking space on the next row, Brandon took off on a dead run. Before the van even came to a complete stop, Brandon was pulling on Dad's door handle. It made no difference, though, since Dad always locks everything. All it did was make Brandon frustrated.

"Dad!" Brandon called through the closed window. "We saw that guy again!"

Dad turned off the engine and opened the door.

"Do you have the letter with you?" Brandon asked, looking frantically into the van. "The one to B. Wright?"

Dad lifted up his blue notebook from between the front seats and said, "It's right here."

"Come here! Quick!" Brandon said, motioning for them both to follow him over to the car where I was standing. "We found a car from Ohio that has a copy of Elias Franzen's document on the front seat!"

"Are you serious?" Mom asked.

"And you can read the note along the edge," Brandon added.

Mom and Dad followed Brandon quickly over to the car and looked through the window.

"That's amazing," Dad whispered. "I think I better call the FBI about this one"

At this point I couldn't decide whether to argue or not, so I didn't say anything. I figured Dad probably wouldn't buy into the idea that maybe this *was* the FBI agent and that he was up to no good. I just watched as he opened up his blue notebook and wrote down the license plate number of the car.

"Did you write down that it's a putrid green Ford Taurus?" I asked.

"I just wrote *green*," Dad said, closing his notebook. "Let's all go to the room and I'll make the call."

"But it *is* putrid, don't you think?" I asked.

"I want to stay here," Brandon said flatly.

Dad looked like he didn't think that was such a great idea. "Why?" he asked.

"Because I want to find out who this guy really is!" Brandon explained. "I think it might be the guy who's missing. Maybe he wasn't really kidnapped after all—maybe he just disappeared on purpose so that he could come steal our treasure!"

"What?" Dad said in total disbelief. "Brandon! First of all, the only one who ever said the word *kidnap,* is *you!* And secondly, it's not *our* treasure—even if there *is* a treasure."

Brandon looked hurt.

Dad drew a deep breath and said a little more calmly, "Let's just all go back to the room and I'll call the FBI."

Brandon was definitely not excited by the idea, but he finally agreed to go. I think it was a good thing we went when we did, too, because the little guys weren't doing too well. I heard both Danny and Chelsea scream when Dad inserted the card and opened the door.

"What's going on in here?" Mom asked as we all came inside the room. Brandon was the last one in and shut the door quickly behind us.

"We're scared!" Danny said with huge eyes. He and Chelsea were hiding behind the sofa.

"Of what?" Dad asked. "What are you doing back there?"

"That man with long hair and the big hat," Chelsea explained. She looked as scared as Danny.

Danny said, "And we thought that he got Jeff and Brandon!" He panted several times, showing exactly how scared he really was.

"We should get a room on the second floor," said Chelsea, "or else on the third floor."

"Why?" Mom asked.

"Because," answered Chelsea, "then we only have to be afraid of the bad man coming in through the door and not through the windows! If our room was on the second floor or on the third floor, then he couldn't get in."

"What if he climbed up?" asked Meg.

Danny drew a huge breath and said loudly, "No! He wouldn't have to climb if he had one of those flying hippos!" We all just stared at him until he continued. "Like in that book that Dad read to us. If he had a flying hippo, then he could get into a window clear up at the top of a tower in a castle—and *nothing* would keep him out!"

"Oh, yeah!" Chelsea said, still with wide eyes. "And if he could go back in time, then he could break in through the window before we got back and our letter would be *gone!*"

This was followed by dead silence, but both Chelsea and Danny were completely into it.

"What are you guys talking about?" I finally said.

"Guys!" Meg giggled. "That stuff isn't true!"

Shauna turned to Dad and said, "Dad, I think you better start choosing books to read to them that are a little closer to reality."

I said, "Right now I think it's partly Brandon's fault for being so frantic about everything."

"What?" Brandon said. "I'm just being careful with things and trying to figure out what's going on! Don't blame me!"

Finally Dad rescued the situation by throwing his hands up in the air and saying, "Whoa! Whoa! Whoa! Everybody settle down!" Motioning for Chelsea and Danny to come out of their hiding spot, he sat down on the sofa with an arm around each of them. "You two don't need to worry about anything." They both looked up into his face without saying anything. "Somebody big from our family will be with you all the time, so you'll always be safe, okay?"

"Okay," they both nodded. Chelsea snuggled in closer and smiled.

"But aren't you going to call the FBI about that car?" Brandon asked, still sounding a little uptight.

"In a minute," said Dad.

"What car?" asked Shauna.

"Jeff and I found a car in the parking lot that has a copy of Elias Franzen's document sitting right on the front seat!" Brandon said.

"And its license plates are from Ohio," I added.

"No way!" Shauna breathed in disbelief.

"Really?" Meg asked. "Do you think it's the missing man?"

"It's the Granite Guy!" Brandon said with mystery in his voice.

"Brandon!" Mom said under her breath. "No more."

Brandon got a shocked and hurt look on his face like he had no clue what she could possibly be referring to. He threw his hands slightly out to the sides and mouthed the word, "*What?*"

Mom just scowled at him in a way that said she knew he knew *exactly* what she meant. Then, in an effort to change the subject she said, "Let's make some lunch, shall we?"

"I want to go back to the pool," Brandon said quickly and quietly.

"Why?" asked Mom.

"I know why," I said. "He wants to keep an eye on that car in the parking lot."

"What's wrong with that?" Brandon asked defensively.

Mom heaved a sigh. "Nothing, I suppose," she said after a moment. "As long as someone goes with you."

"I'll go!" said Danny. I guess he wasn't feeling scared anymore. Chelsea, on the other hand, looked like she was perfectly content to stay snuggled up to Dad on the couch.

"I meant someone older," Mom said, turning to me and Shauna.

I figured Shauna wouldn't want to, so I volunteered. "But Brandon has to promise not to do anything dumb," I said, copying Shauna's idea from earlier.

"Good point," Mom said.

"I *won't*," Brandon said.

"You won't promise?" I asked.

Brandon smirked.

As we headed out the door, Brandon said to Dad, "Don't forget to call the FBI."

"I won't," Dad said with a deep breath. I don't think he felt like he needed a reminder.

As soon as we got back into the pool area Brandon started craning his neck to make sure the car with the copy of the missing document was still there. It was parked a couple of rows away from where we were, so it was hard to see for sure.

"I can't see it anymore!" Brandon said. He was getting frantic again. It was getting a little old. "The car's gone!" he yelled.

"Are you sure?" I asked.

Without bothering to answer, Brandon took off on a dead run again, crashing through the gate that led from the pool area out into the parking lot.

Danny looked up at me and said, "Is Brandon doing something dumb now?"

I nodded my head a couple of times before sighing and saying, "He's doing his best."

"So should we go with him?" Danny asked. "Do you think Mom would want us to go with him?"

"Probably," I sighed.

Not moving nearly as quickly as Brandon did, Danny and I started toward the parking lot. Just as the gate slammed shut I heard Brandon yell, "It's gone!" I looked over in his direction and saw him throw his hands up in disgust. "We *lost* him!" Brandon called.

Danny and I didn't bother to go over to witness the empty parking spot for ourselves, choosing instead to just wait at the sidewalk until Brandon decided to make his way slowly back. First, though, he spent at least a full minute scanning all the cars in both directions on the road in front of the hotel. The guy was obviously long gone.

We made our way back to our family's room now, since there was no longer any reason to be out by the pool. Danny still wanted to swim, of course, but we convinced him to come have some lunch first.

The first thing Brandon said when we got back to the room was, "Did you call the FBI?"

Dad answered, "I did. They said that they didn't have anyone in the area, but they would have a local police officer come by to check it out."

"Call them back and tell them not to bother," Brandon said with sadness. "The car is gone."

"Well," said Dad, "they wanted to get some more information from us, too, so we'll just tell them that when they get here."

Brandon mumbled something, but I didn't quite catch it.

Nobody really said anything more about it as we finished making and eating lunch. It was obvious that Brandon was pretty discouraged, because he didn't say anything more about *anything*. He just ate in silence, chewing each bite forever.

After lunch we all went swimming. Mom and Dad even played Marco Polo with us, but Mom made us change the name of it to be more consistent with our vacation. At first we were trying to pick a name of somebody famous from the Rock and Roll Hall of Fame, but we could never agree on which name to use. So finally we decided to use the name "Blaine Wright." Other people at the pool thought we were a little strange calling "Blaine" and answering "Wright" instead of "Marco" and "Polo." But we didn't care. The funny looks that we got just made it that much more fun.

At one point during the game Shauna came over to where Brandon and I were. Chelsea was "it" and she was clear at the other end of the pool.

"Hey, guys," Shauna whispered. "I know how we can find out if that long-haired man is the FBI agent."

"How?" Brandon asked, very interested.

"We can record his voice on my computer and see if it matches," Shauna smiled.

"See if it matches *what?*" Brandon asked. "Don't you need another recording to match it with?"

"I have one!" Shauna beamed. "Remember the day those FBI guys first showed up at our house? I was in the middle of recording when they came in and I forgot to stop it."

"No way!" said Brandon. "That's *great!*"

"How are we ever going to get close enough get another recording?" I asked.

"I don't know," Shauna said, "but the guy keeps showing up places. If we just keep our eyes open we might get a chance."

It seemed like a long shot to me, but Brandon really liked the idea. That's all that was said about it, though, because we suddenly realized that Chelsea was really close and so we all scattered. I noticed that Brandon seemed to be having fun, forgetting at least for a little while about the car vanishing before he could show it to the police or the FBI. But as we were drying off and getting ready to go back to the room he said, "The police never came."

"No, they didn't," Dad said.

"Maybe they did," Meg suggested, "but we missed them because we were having so much fun playing."

"I told them that we would either be in our room or at the pool," Dad said. "Agent Smith told me that he would be sure to pass that on to the local police, so they should have gotten the message."

"I never should have left the parking lot," Brandon mumbled.

"Why not?" Mom asked. "What were you planning to do if someone came out to get in the car?"

"I don't know," Brandon said, rubbing his hair with his towel. "Something."

"I think I'm glad not to know," Dad said. "But don't worry about it. Things will work out. They always do."

Brandon opened his mouth to say something, but then thought better of it.

"Why do we have to stop swimming now?" Danny asked.

"Because," Mom said with excitement. She reached over and dried his ears with her towel. "We're going to see some really neat places in Palmyra this afternoon."

"Like what?" Chelsea asked.

Mom said, "Like the Sacred Grove, where Heavenly Father and Jesus Christ first appeared to Joseph Smith."

"Really?" said Danny.

"Yep," said Dad. "And the home where he was living when the angel Moroni appeared to him."

"We are?" asked Chelsea.

"And the Hill Cumorah," said Mom. "That's where the gold plates were buried before Joseph Smith got them."

"Let's go!" yelled Danny, taking off through the gate and heading back to our room.

As we all walked back toward the room Dad asked, "Do you remember what scripture Moroni quoted to Joseph Smith after he first told him about the gold plates?"

None of us did. Well, Mom probably did—she had a big smile on her face.

"What scripture were we looking for last night?" Dad asked. "The one that we found in all the standard works?"

"Oh, yeah," said Shauna, "the one about turning the hearts of the fathers to the children and the children to the fathers."

"The sealing power is a big deal, isn't it?" I said.

"Yes, it is," Dad agreed. "It's one of the greatest blessings of this dispensation."

We walked in silence the rest of the way back to the room.

The rest of the afternoon and evening was great. I loved seeing the old homes where Joseph Smith's family had lived. It was especially neat to see the upstairs room where Joseph had been sleeping the night that Moroni appeared to him three times. I decided that since Moroni said almost the exact same words each of the three times, it must all be pretty important. I stayed behind in that room for a few minutes after the rest of my family went back downstairs. I was just trying to take it all in. I was trying to imagine what that must have been like for Joseph Smith.

The best place we visited that afternoon, though, was the Sacred Grove. It was in a forested area with trails winding this way and that way all through the grove. Near the base of one of the trees we found a marker that estimated how old the tree was. From the estimate, it looked like the tree could have been there at the same time Joseph Smith's family was living nearby.

The grove really wasn't very big, but we spent about an hour, walking under the trees and sitting together for a time, talking quietly about what had happened there. It was such a peaceful place and there was such a spirit there that it felt like being in a chapel. Along the trails here and there we found benches. Many of them were being used by people who were resting or praying or reading scriptures. It was really cool.

Just down the road from the grove was the Palmyra Temple, where Mom and Dad had done a session earlier in the day.

"How was it?" Shauna asked.

"It was nice," Dad said. "The feeling is a little different in the smaller temples than in the big ones, but the Spirit is always strong, no matter which temple you're in."

"What are we going to do now?" asked Chelsea.

"We're going to see the Hill Cumorah Pageant," said Mom.

"What's that?" Chelsea asked.

Mom said, "It's a show put on by hundreds of people that tells about the Book of Mormon—how we got it and what's in it."

"And it's outside," said Dad, "on the side of the hill where the gold plates were buried."

"Shall we get something to eat before we go?" Mom asked.

"I was thinking," Dad said, "that maybe we could go over now and get seats and then some of us could go get some dinner and bring it back."

"Okay," Mom nodded, as we climbed into the van. "I didn't see too many fast food places around, though."

Brandon grabbed the opportunity to vote for what he wanted. "I saw a Pizza Hut on the way here!" he said.

"That's true," Dad nodded, "we did pass one about ten minutes before we got to Palmyra."

"Is pizza okay with everyone?" Mom asked, turning around in her seat.

Everyone agreed—or at least no one disagreed. Shauna just smiled.

We were a couple of hours early for the pageant, but half the chairs sprawling across the huge lawn were already taken. There must have been thousands of people there. Dad took Meg, Chelsea, and Danny with him to go get the pizza, while the rest of us stayed behind to save our seats. Luckily, Mom had thought to have us bring our backpacks in the van, so we all had something to read or whatever while we waited. We didn't get much of a chance, though, because not long after we sat down, the cast members came out and began walking around and talking to everyone in the audience.

It turned out that the members of the cast came from all over the United States to be in the pageant. Some of them had come every year for a long time. Some came by themselves and others came with their whole families. Apparently, if you wanted to be in the pageant, you had to commit to be there for a total of at least three weeks for rehearsals and then the performances. I thought it was cool that some people were able to take their families for that long.

There were buses that would bring the people every day from where they were staying so they could rehearse. They had huge tents covering long tables where they would all eat together. They even had some days where they would do community service for the people or the town of Palmyra—most of whom are not members of the Church. The whole thing seemed pretty amazing to me.

The cast members were all very friendly, and we had a great time talking to them until one of the men told us that he was from Ohio. Brandon immediately got *very* suspicious of him and started asking all sorts of questions.

"What kind of car do you drive?" Brandon asked.

The man just stared at him. "It's a van," he said after a moment.

"What do you know about old documents?" Brandon asked.

The man looked confused.

"What part of Ohio are you from?"

"C-C-Columbus," the man answered.

"Right," Brandon said, as though he didn't believe him. "Why did you hesitate?"

The man just stared at him like he couldn't believe what was happening. "Because you're acting like a policeman!" the man said.

"Do you have experience with the police?" Brandon asked.

"Brandon!" Mom said. She had been talking with someone else and only heard the last couple of comments. The man excused himself and found someone else to talk to who was several rows away from us. I noticed that he kept glancing back in our direction.

Brandon defended himself by saying, "Hey, the guy *admitted* he was from Ohio!"

"Of course he did," Mom said. "Because there's nothing *wrong* with being from Ohio!"

"Get a grip, Brandon!" I said.

101

Luckily, Dad showed up with the pizzas about then. If there's anything in the world that can bring Brandon back to reality, it's pizza. I'm sure he'd eat it for every meal every day if he could. I figured that he probably looked forward to being a grown-up for that reason alone.

After we had had enough pizza, Brandon and I asked Dad if we could go to the parking area and throw a Frisbee for a while. The cars were all parked in a big grassy field that looked like a perfect Frisbee spot. And from where we were, it looked like at least half of the field was still open.

"Be back before it's dark," Mom said. "The show starts as soon as it gets dark."

"We will," Brandon said.

I guess I should have known that Brandon had more on his mind than Frisbee. As soon as we got across the street to where the cars were parked, Brandon said, "Jeff, let's see if that same car from Ohio is here! I'll bet it is!"

I wasn't really interested in checking out every single car. I had just eaten way too much pizza. We checked every car on every row, though, and it wasn't there. Brandon seemed disappointed, but I was relieved. I was tired of worrying about this crazy guy. I figured that with his big hat and all that hair, he would be easy enough to spot. We threw the Frisbee for a while and then made our way back to our seats.

The pageant started just about the time we got back. It was probably the most incredible production I have ever seen. The stage was huge and there were speakers everywhere, so it was really easy to hear and understand everything that was going on. The show moved really fast and had some really awesome special effects. There were flashes of fire and downpours of rain. When they were telling the part about Christ appearing in America they even made it look like he just appeared in the sky and then gradually came down to earth. He went up again the same way. It was amazing.

After the show Mom and Dad were in no hurry to leave. And that was okay with me. They had done a great job and it was nice to feel the spirit that was there. We sat around and talked about our favorite scenes from the show for at least fifteen or twenty minutes before finally gathering up our backpacks and empty pizza boxes and heading for the car.

"That was a very peaceful ending to a crazy day," I said to anyone who might be listening.

CHAPTER 9

Roots

Sunday morning we went to church in Rochester, New York. We were pretty much used to the Eastern time zone by now and church didn't start till 9:30. There was a ward building only three miles (estimated time: five minutes) from our hotel. Dad's book of directions took us straight to it (unlike the last Sunday) and so we were actually on time. After church we went back to our hotel for lunch and then headed out for the afternoon to see more Church history sights that we hadn't seen the day before. We saw Martin Harris's farm—the one that he mortgaged to pay for the first printing of the Book of Mormon. We also saw the building and printing shop where the first edition of the Book of Mormon was printed by a man named E. B. Grandin. That was probably my favorite place that afternoon.

In the evening, after we came back to our hotel for dinner, we had a family devotional.

"One more time," Dad said, "what is the theme of our family vacation?"

"Family history!" Chelsea said with excitement.

"Right!" smiled Dad.

"Genealogy," added Shauna.

"Same thing," said Dad. "Good job."

"Roots!" Meg said.

Dad looked over at Meg with a surprised half-smile and said slowly, "Right. And above the roots grows what?"

"Our family tree?" Meg asked.

"A tree!" nodded Dad. "Tonight we're going to talk about the tree of life. Who knows where we find it?"

"First Nephi," Brandon said.

"Chapter and verse?" Dad asked.

Brandon scrunched up his face as he tried to remember.

Dad got a strange look on his face and said, "It sort of makes you wish the Book of Mormon had an index, doesn't it?"

"But it *does* have an index," Meg said with a confused look on her face.

"He knows that," Brandon said with a smirk. "That's just Dad's way of saying, 'Duh! Use the index!' Isn't it, Dad?"

Dad just smiled.

Well, it didn't take long to find the story of Lehi's and Nephi's vision in chapters 8 and 11 of 1 Nephi. We spent at least the next hour each drawing our own tree of life and writing down what everything meant. It was really pretty fun. Dad even had colored pencils and markers that we could use if we wanted.

About halfway through drawing her picture, Meg asked, "Where do the roots of the tree go?"

We found nothing about roots in the description, but we decided that even though the roots are in the ground and you can't see them, they bring the living water to the tree and give it life.

"Just like we can't see the people who are the roots of our family tree," Meg beamed. "But we're all connected."

"Oh, yeah," Shauna said. "And we need each other, huh? Just like the leaves bring in light for the tree, we can bring Light to our family tree."

"Remember," Mom said, "if we don't have the sealing power to connect us all together, then the earth is cursed—its whole purpose is lost."

Monday morning Dad didn't let us sleep in. He wanted to get to Niagara Falls. We ate breakfast in the lobby, packed, and were on the road by ten o'clock. It only took about an hour and a half to get there. As we were crossing a huge bridge high above the river below, Dad called back, "There's Canada!"

None of us had ever been to Canada before. There were all sorts of buildings and roads covering the hillside on the other side of the river.

"What city is that?" Brandon asked.

"That's Niagara Falls," Dad said.

"I thought Niagara Falls was some huge waterfall!" I said, slightly confused.

"It is," Mom said. "That's the *city* of Niagara Falls. But if you look out there," she said, pointing out the left side of the van, "you'll see the waterfalls."

I think Niagara Falls is the most amazing natural sight I've ever seen. The river was split in two, creating two huge waterfalls. The American Falls on the left looked like a very steep mountainside with water gushing down over it. The Canadian Falls, on the right, had all the old broken up rocks and boulders taken away from the bottom, so the water fell pretty much straight down, making a huge cloud of mist and spray that billowed up from the river. It was incredible.

While waiting in line to pull up to a booth where the Canadian border patrol was checking cars through, we all crowded next to the windows on the left side of the van and said, "Whoa!" or "That's amazing!" and things like that.

"Can we go over closer to it?" Chelsea asked.

"We are going to get right in it!" Mom said.

"Wait, what?" Shauna asked. "How?"

"See those boats down there?" Mom asked, pointing at the river below the falls. "They'll take us right into the mist of the Canadian Falls."

106

There was a dock on the Canadian side of the river that had several boats tied up next to it. I noticed that one of the boats was already about halfway from the dock to the cloud of water.

"Check it out!" I said. "That boat's going in there right now."

We all watched for the next couple of minutes as the boat got closer and closer to the falls. The closer the boat got, the harder it was to see. Eventually, we couldn't see it at all.

We all started chattering with excitement.

"When are we going?" Danny asked with enthusiasm.

"This afternoon," said Dad.

"Won't we get wet?" Meg asked.

"They give everyone a poncho to wear," Mom explained. "See how everyone on that boat down there is wearing bright blue."

She was right, but none of us had noticed it before.

After Dad told the border patrol officer that we would be staying in Canada one night and that we were here for sight-seeing, he let us drive through the gate. We went straight to the hotel to check in. This one didn't have suites, so we were going to be split up in two rooms for this one night—it was like having a boy's dorm and a girl's dorm. I went inside with Mom and Dad.

"I guess this place has an inside pool," I said as we entered the lobby. I could smell the chlorine as soon as we got inside.

"I think you're right!" Dad nodded.

When we were all checked in, the lady behind the desk told us to drive around the back where there was a parking lot right next to the elevators.

"Guess what, Danny," I said as we climbed back into the van.

"What?" he asked, without any interest.

"This hotel has an indoor swimming pool," I said.

"It *does?*" Danny asked, now with excitement. Then he asked, "Is our room close to it?"

"We're up on the sixth floor," Mom said. "But the lady said that the pool is really close to the elevators."

Danny said he figured that was pretty okay.

When we got around to the back of the hotel, we saw something that made my heart jump: there was a man with long, brown hair and a large, yellowish straw hat going into the hotel. I couldn't see if he had a beard or not because his back was to us.

"Look!" Brandon almost shouted. "There's the Granite Guy!"

"You mean Agent Sniff," I corrected him. "And there's the putrid green car from our hotel parking lot."

Parked right in front of the back door into the hotel was a car that looked exactly the same as the one we had seen before. It was parked right behind a big van that had the hotel's name printed across the back doors.

"You're right!" said Brandon.

"No, he's not," Dad said. "This one has New York license plates—not Ohio."

Brandon eyes got big. "He *stole* them!" Brandon breathed.

"Oh!" Dad scoffed. "There are lots of green Ford Tauruses around."

"Not that have that funny peace sign in the back window," Brandon said. He was right. I hadn't really thought about it at the time, but this car had the same peace sign sticker in the window.

"He's right, Dad!" I said with excitement. "I remember it, too!"

"Dad!" said Shauna suddenly. "Park right behind it so he can't get away."

"What?" said Dad in disbelief.

"Dad, do it!" Shauna said. "If nobody's here when the guy comes out, then he'll go into the front desk and tell them to move their van. If I can record his voice when he goes to the desk, then maybe I can find out who he is!"

The thought made chills run up my spine. "I'll go with you, Shauna," I said quickly.

"I think this is something we should leave to the FBI or the police," Dad said.

"But they are doing *nothing* to help!" Brandon said. "They didn't even show up when they could have gotten the license plate number."

"Shauna, I don't think anyone's going to put much faith into your friend's experimental voice-matching software," said Dad.

"But if we can get a *recording*," Shauna pleaded, "then they can analyze it any way they want to!"

"If this guy *is* a criminal," Brandon said, "then he's now crossed *international* boundaries!"

"Dad, park quick," Shauna urged, "so we can all be gone when he comes back out."

"That's a red curb," Dad said in amazement. "I can't park there!"

"Dad!" Brandon practically yelled. "You're missing the whole point!"

"C'mon, Dad!" I pleaded. "For *once* in your life—*park* next to a *red curb!* If I'd thought of it before, *that's* what I would have chosen instead of the Hard Rock Café! *Please!*"

We all waited for at least two full seconds of tense silence.

"Okay," Dad finally sighed.

"Yes!" Shauna clenched her fists with excitement. She pulled her computer from her bag and pressed the power button as Dad pulled forward to box in the putrid green car.

"Let's go, Jeff," Shauna called as she pushed the van door open and jumped out onto the sidewalk.

"Everybody else get out, too!" Brandon yelled.

"Where do you think we're going to go?" Mom asked. Neither she nor Dad seemed to appreciate what a great opportunity this was.

As I jumped out I heard Dad say, "I guess we could take the bags up to our room."

"Okay, but hurry!" Brandon yelled.

As I ran past the car in front of us, I slowed down long enough to see if the document was still sitting on the front seat. I didn't see the document, but I was still sure that we had the right guy. I ran through the hotel door after Shauna.

Once inside the hotel, we moved cautiously just in case the man with the hat was around somewhere. We didn't see him by the elevators, so we moved quickly into the lobby that stretched all the way to the front of the hotel. The entire back portion of the lobby area was taken up by a pretty good sized swimming pool with a low, wrought iron fence around it. As we walked past it, I noticed that the smell of chlorine was even stronger here than up by the front desk where we had come in. The surface of the water was completely smooth. The rest of the lobby held a large eating area filled with tables, chairs, and benches where I figured they probably served breakfast each morning. The lady had said that breakfast was free, but she never mentioned where we had to go to get it. I scanned both the pool and eating areas as we went past, looking for the man. As we made our way toward the front desk, Shauna was punching buttons on her computer, trying to get it ready to record. I was on the lookout in all directions, just in case the guy showed up.

"C'mon, c'mon, c'mon!" Shauna mumbled intently, waiting for the computer to finish booting up.

We got to the front desk and just stood there for a moment, watching the computer screen.

"It's almost ready," Shauna whispered.

"May I help you?" asked the lady behind the counter.

I looked up in surprise. "O-oh, no, thanks," I smiled weakly. "We—uh—we're just w-waiting for someone."

"Very well," said the lady. "My name is Annie. Please let me know if I can do anything for you." Then she went back into the office.

"Okay," whispered Shauna. "Should I start it now?"

"No," I said. "Let's wait till we see him."

"Should I just stand here?" she asked. "I don't want to just stand here."

I thought for a moment and said, "No, when he comes we can just leave it on the desk and go over there." I gestured toward the tables and benches.

"Okay," she said. She seemed really nervous. And she was making *me* nervous, too.

We stood at the desk for at least three or four minutes. I noticed that the back side of one of the elevators was glass and you could see inside it for the bottom three stories as it went up or down. We saw Dad, Meg, and Chelsea get into it with a bunch of luggage.

"Do you think everyone else is still at the van?" I asked, annoyed at the thought. "They need to hurry."

"Maybe they already went up in the other elevator," Shauna suggested.

"Maybe," I agreed, but I wasn't convinced.

After the elevator disappeared from view, the lady came out and said, "Still waiting?"

We just smiled nervously and nodded.

A couple more minutes went by. Then I saw him. He was coming down in the glass elevator.

"There he is!" I hissed.

"Should I start it?" Shauna asked.

"Yeah! Hurry!" I breathed. "Let's go."

She clicked the record button on the screen and then pulled the lid most of the way down so that no one could see the screen. As we walked away I saw the elevator doors open and the man with the hat step out the other side. By the time he came around the corner and started walking through the lobby toward the front desk, Shauna and I were almost all the way to the back of the eating area. We were too nervous to sit, so we just stood facing each other, making nervous glances toward the front desk. The lady came out

111

of the office and the two began speaking, but we were too far away to hear what they were saying.

"This is so great!" I whispered. "We're gonna nail this guy!"

"I hope so!" Shauna whispered back. She gave a small shudder. I figured she must have been *really* nervous.

We watched the man gesture toward the back door.

"It's working!" I said. "He's doing exactly what you thought he would! You're good!"

Shauna just smiled back.

The lady behind the desk looked in the direction of the back doors and then picked up the phone and made a quick call. She smiled at him after she hung up and then he started to walk away. I figured she must have called someone to go move the hotel van. Then the man stopped short and came back to the counter. He said something to the woman and she put the phone up on the counter for him to use. He dialed a number and began speaking into the phone.

"What's he doing?" I asked. "This isn't part of your plan!"

Shauna just looked at me.

"How long will the recording go?" I asked.

"Fifteen minutes," Shauna said.

The man hung up after just a minute or so and headed for the back of the hotel again. As he walked away, Shauna and I pretended to be deep in conversation.

"He's gone," Shauna said after a moment, and headed straight for her computer. She pulled open the lid and clicked the stop button. "Good," she said. "We got three minutes and forty-three seconds."

"So do the matching," I said.

"Are you still waiting for someone?" asked the lady behind the counter. She had come out of the office again without us noticing and we both jumped. Shauna almost dropped the computer.

"Oh!" said the lady. "I apologize for startling you!"

"It's all right," Shauna breathed. "No, I think we're going up to our room now. Maybe they're still up there."

"Very well," smiled the woman.

Shauna closed the computer and headed for the elevators. All the way up to the sixth floor and down the hall to our room I tried to get Shauna to do the voice matching, but she wanted to wait until we got to our room. If we had known where our room was, it wouldn't have been so bad. But Dad never told us the room number, so we just stood halfway down the hall on the sixth floor waiting for some sign from someone we knew.

"I don't think this was part of your plan either, was it?" I asked.

Shauna ignored me.

After a couple of minutes Dad and Danny came out of a room a few doors down from where we were standing.

"Down here," Dad said. As we got closer, he asked, "How did it go?"

"We got three minutes and forty-three seconds," I said, "but she hasn't run the match yet."

"How long does it take?" Dad asked.

"Just a few seconds," Shauna said. "A lot less time than the recording lasts. It compresses everything."

"Danny and I are going to go move the van from the red curb," Dad said. "You can tell us what you found when we get back."

I couldn't believe it. He was so uptight about the red curb that he couldn't even wait five more minutes. We got Brandon from the boy's room and all went into the girl's room together. Mom already had Meg and Chelsea unpacking.

"Run the matching," I said as soon as the door closed.

Shauna opened the computer and made a few clicks. Brandon and I had seen this before, so we leaned over her shoulders, watching the screen.

"Shauna the Beautiful matched at seventy-two percent, didn't it?" Brandon asked. "How high do you think this one will be?"

Shauna ignored the question, probably because she didn't appreciate the little reminder. After a few seconds a message popped up on the computer screen that read, "No matches."

"*What?*" I said in disbelief. "So it's *not* Agent Tassle-Shoes?"

"I *knew* it!" Brandon said with a smug look. "It's *got* to be Granite Guy!"

Shauna shook her head. "It's not him either," she said.

Brandon looked shocked and hurt. "What do you mean?" he asked.

"You don't have a recording of *his* voice," I said.

"Yes, I do," Shauna nodded. "Remember: Dad played that voice mail message when the FBI guys were there, and I recorded everything. I have both the FBI agents in here and the man on the phone, too."

"It's not him?" Brandon asked, still in disbelief.

"So who is it then?" Dad asked, coming into the room. He looked much more relaxed now that the van was no longer parked next to a red curb.

"We have no idea," Shauna said.

CHAPTER 10

Under Niagara Falls

"I really thought it was Agent Smith," I said dejectedly to Dad, "but it wasn't."

"And it wasn't the guy from the archives, either," said Brandon.

"How do you know?" Dad said.

"Because," explained Shauna, "the day the FBI agents came to our house the computer recorded the whole conversation. Remember when you played the voice mail message? I got his voice from that. I also have both of the agents' voices, as well as everybody in our family."

"Well, I'm glad to hear that it's no one in our family," Dad said with a wry smile. "I'd hate to think that we were stalking ourselves!"

He laughed at his own words. But no one else seemed to think there was anything funny about it.

"Dad," I said seriously, shaking my head slightly, "why do you laugh at your own jokes when no one else does?"

Still chuckling slightly, Dad said thoughtfully, "I guess I'm just trying to prime the pump! You know what that means, don't you?"

"Yes," said Meg, "you think that we might laugh at something that's not *at all* funny, if you laugh at it first."

Dad's smile faded quickly now and he said, "I guess that's *one* way to put it."

Changing the subject, Mom asked, "Is everything in from the van?"

"Yes," answered Dad. "*And* it's parked in a legitimate parking stall!"

"Congratulations, Dad," Brandon said. "But didn't it feel good to be parked by a red curb just for a few minutes? Didn't it make you feel exhilarated and alive?"

Dad looked at Brandon like he couldn't believe he was serious. "No!" he said emphatically. "It made me feel nervous and guilty."

Brandon just stared back at him.

"What if the hotel had a strict tow-on-sight policy?" Dad asked, completely seriously. "What if the van ended up in some impound yard and I had to pay big Canadian bucks to get it out and then they wouldn't give it to us because it was a rental and not registered in my name? And what if . . . ?"

"Dad!" Shauna said. "It's okay! We get the picture: you didn't like it! We won't ask you to do it again."

"Thanks," Dad mumbled. "I'd appreciate it."

"And we won't ask you about it again, either," Shauna said. "Right, Brandon? Because we don't want Dad to have to relive his pain and anguish anymore."

Once Dad finally rejoined reality, we agreed to quickly eat some sandwiches and then head out. Mom, of course, wanted to go to the front desk first and find out everything she possibly could about things to do in less than twenty-four hours in Niagara Falls. Dad and Shauna stood at the counter with her as she asked the hotel lady tons of questions about things that kids would like the best, which tours of the Falls were the best, and the best places to eat. The rest of us sat around some tables in the eating area of the hotel—all of us except Danny, that is. He was standing at the iron gate by the pool, watching the quiet water.

"Let's go, Daniel!" Dad called to Danny after a few minutes, who came running to where the rest of us were.

Dad started toward the front doors of the lobby.

"Aren't we taking the van?" Brandon asked.

"Nope," Dad said. "Apparently there's not really anyplace to park that's closer than the hotel, so we're just going to walk."

"And besides that," smiled Mom, "there are a few places along the way where we absolutely *have* to stop."

"Like the Hershey's Chocolate Store?" Shauna asked with bright eyes.

"Well, of course," smiled Mom as she headed out the door. "They give free samples!"

The sun was really bright outside.

"Whoa!" Brandon said. "I shouldn't have left my sunglasses in the room."

"I think mine are there, too," I said, squinting.

"Dad," Brandon said, "can we go back to the room for our sunglasses?"

"Why didn't you get a hat like everyone else did when I told you to?" Dad asked.

I was surprised by the question. "Sorry," I said, "I guess I didn't hear you."

"Me, either," agreed Brandon.

"Hurry," Dad said, handing Brandon the access card. "We'll be going down the street this direction," he said, pointing.

Brandon and I ran back through the lobby, rode the elevators to the sixth floor, and got our sunglasses as quickly as we could. Back outside the hotel we could see the rest of the family about a block ahead and took off running in their direction. It was a hot day and so even that short distance was enough to make me feel sweaty.

"I'm hot," I said to Brandon, panting. "I can hardly wait to get drenched. Maybe I won't wear one of those ponchos."

We turned the corner and found that though the street we had been walking on was fairly level, this street was quite steep for all three blocks, leading down to the river. This was an interesting

117

place with people and shops everywhere. There were groups here and there wearing matching blue or yellow ponchos. Apparently, they had recently been on boat rides under the Falls. I couldn't figure out if they were planning to go again or if they were just enjoying being wrapped up in cheap, clingy plastic.

We stopped at a few places and saw some pretty cool stuff, but by far my favorite place was the Hershey's store. They had free samples, all right. Each person could get chunks of at least six different kinds of fudge. It's a good thing Mom had made Danny eat a sandwich before we went there, otherwise I'm sure he would have made himself sick—he kept going back to the free sample place more times than I could count. My favorite was the peanut butter fudge. Brandon liked the strawberry cheesecake fudge, because it didn't taste anything like chocolate. Can it really be fudge if there's no chocolate in it?

We finally got down to the river about mid-afternoon. The sky had clouded over and the air had cooled off quite a bit. When we got to the ticket office the man in the booth said, "You came at a good time. The lines always drop way down when it looks like rain." He handed Dad the tickets and said, "It's somewhat silly, though, because you're going to get a lot more wet on the boat ride than you'd ever get from a little rain."

"Really?" Mom asked.

The man smiled and said, "Keep those ponchos on!"

From the ticket office we rode an elevator down to the dock and got in a line for ponchos. There were only two sizes: child and adult. Chelsea and Danny both got the small ones. My poncho hung just past my knees, but Meg's went all the way to the ground.

We got onboard, and as the boat pulled away from the dock and headed for the Canadian Falls, a voice over the loudspeaker on the boat started telling us some of the history of the Falls. They told some cool stories about the people who had actually gone over the Falls and survived. But they said that most people who went over the Falls either on purpose or by accident were killed. They also said that the Falls keep moving back as more and more rocks break off and fall into the river below. It made me wonder if someday the city of Niagara Falls wouldn't be next to Niagara Falls anymore.

The closer we got to the cloud of mist and spray, the tighter everyone started to pull their ponchos around themselves. Danny figured out that if he pulled his hood down completely over his face that he could still see through the plastic—it just made everything blue! There were two levels on the boat. Most people had crowded up on the top level near the front of the boat. We were along the side near the back when the captain of the boat came up the stairs from the lower deck.

The captain came over by us and said, "If you want to see where we're going, the lower deck is practically empty, and you can get up near the front of the boat."

I turned to Brandon and asked, "Should we do it, Bran?"

"You'll get quite a bit more wet down there, too," the captain smiled.

That was all we needed to hear. We told Mom and Dad where we were headed and immediately hopped down the stairs. The captain was right: there were only a handful of people down there and already we could tell that it was a lot wetter. We figured it was probably because we were closer to the splashing river. Brandon and I leaned against the guardrail near the front of the boat. All we could see in front of us was a huge white cloud. More and more it was starting to feel like we were in a downpour.

By the time we got into the cloud, I was sure that I had never been so wet in all my life. There was so much water that I could barely keep my eyes open. And when I did, I could barely see Brandon, let alone anything else. It was like standing under 12 showerheads at the same time! Water was running down our faces like—like we were at the bottom of a huge waterfall!

It was loud, too. Brandon and I had to yell to be heard above the noise. Eventually we just quit trying and stood there in the downpour for several minutes. Finally it started to let up. When I looked around I couldn't see where Brandon had gone. I called out his name a couple of times in the direction of the few people who were on the lower deck, but I couldn't find him. A couple of the people glanced in my direction, but they were too busy laughing and wiping the water from their drenched faces to really pay any attention to me.

Then I heard something that made me grab the guardrail in complete panic. The sound of a siren came blaring over the boat's loudspeaker. It was a burst of noise that started with a low pitch and quickly got louder and higher. There was about a one second break in between each burst of the siren. After the second burst, the captain's voice on the intercom yelled, "Man overboard!" Another burst of the siren. "I repeat!" the captain called again. "Man overboard!"

I looked frantically down into the river, but there was still too much mist and spray for me to really see anything very clearly. I ran back and forth to either side of the boat looking for any sign of Brandon or a blue poncho in the water. The siren continued to blare out in short bursts. As the boat continued to move out of the mist, I heard someone yell, "There he is!"

One of the passengers was pointing into the river just a few feet from the side of the boat. Now everyone was pointing and yelling. I ran to where they stood and saw a huge blue plastic bubble in the water with arms flailing violently over and through it. It was Brandon. He was trying to get the poncho away from his face so he could breathe. A couple of the boat's crew came running down the side of the boat and threw a large, round life preserver in his direction. One of them held tightly onto the long rope that was connected to it. The throw was amazing! The life preserver came to rest about six inches in front of Brandon's face. He saw it and quickly grabbed on.

The flow of the river was carrying us quickly out of the huge cloud and before I even realized it the mist and spray were gone. The crew quickly pulled Brandon in closer to the boat. He was coughing and sputtering, still fighting with the poncho that clung to him like flypaper. One of the crew climbed over the guardrail and partway down the side of the boat, reaching out for Brandon to take his hand. This was the first time I noticed that the deck of the boat was actually only a couple of feet above the surface of the water. Brandon reached toward the crewman and they grabbed each other's wrists. Brandon was quickly out of the water and soon back on the deck of the boat, lying flat on his back with an anxious crowd gathered around. A lot of people from the upper deck had come down to get a better look.

"Give him some room to breathe!" called the crewman. "Stay back, please!" Then to Brandon, he asked quietly, "Are you alright?"

Brandon started to nod, but turned his head quickly to the side as he experienced a series of violent coughs that forced water from his lungs. Finally, he wiped his mouth with his hand and breathed, "I'm fine." Putting his arm across his eyes he said, "But it's bright."

The sun had come out again and it was warming up fast. Just then Mom and Dad made their way through the crowd that had refused to give Brandon room to breathe. "Are you okay?" Mom asked, kneeling down next to him. She looked him over from top to bottom.

"Yeah," Brandon panted. "I'm all right." He coughed a few more times and tried to sit up.

"Stay down for just a minute more," one of the crewman said. Then to the other one, he called, "Get me a life jacket."

"What happened?" Dad asked. "Did you just slip?"

"I—I'm not sure," Brandon whispered, his head rocking slowly back and forth.

The life jacket was placed under Brandon's head. I'm sure it was a lot more comfortable than the wooden deck. I guessed I probably would have tried to sit up, too, if someone was trying to make me lie on a hard, wooden floor.

"Okay, folks," the crewman called again. "Give us some room here! Give him air!"

About this time the boat pulled up to the dock and people began filing off. I could hear lots of jabbering about what had happened to Brandon and whether he was all right. When people got onto the dock, they would look back over at us, trying to see what was going on.

"Can you tell us what happened?" asked the captain, who was now standing over Brandon. "Did you just slip? Were you leaning over the guardrail?"

"I was sort of leaning against it, I guess," Brandon said. He closed his eyes and looked as though he was trying to remember.

"Then what?" asked the captain. He seemed calm, but intent on finding out exactly what had happened.

"It was when there was water everywhere," Brandon explained slowly. "So I couldn't really see anything. I closed my eyes and just let the water run down my face."

We all waited for Brandon to continue. His eyes were still closed. He reached up and rubbed his forehead with his hand.

"Then . . ." Brandon stammered a little, "it was like my feet just came out from under me." He paused. "I felt myself falling forward." Another pause. "I reached back for the guardrail as I was falling over it and I saw Jeff standing a couple feet away from me with his eyes closed." Brandon coughed again and then screwed up his face like he was trying to figure something out. "It *almost* felt like someone had pushed me, but I never was able to turn around far enough to see if anyone was there." He paused again. "But between being wrapped up in this poncho and the water pouring over me, I just can't be sure."

He opened his eyes and blinked a few times. "Can I sit up now?"

122

Brandon asked. Not only did they let him sit up, but by this time they were ready to kick us all off the boat completely; they had another load of passengers starting to get onboard. There was a small building with an office on the dock. The captain took us here and told us the police would be arriving any minute.

"I don't remember such a thing ever happening before," the captain said. Turning to Brandon, he added, "The police will want to know everything you can remember."

Brandon just nodded.

"Do you need to get back to the boat?" Mom asked the captain.

"No," he said quickly. "There are plenty of others who can take care of the boat. I'll stay with you until the police have finished."

Two police officers were there almost immediately. They asked all the same questions that the captain had. One of the officers wrote down everything Brandon said. Brandon, like all the rest of us, was still wearing his blue poncho. When Brandon said he wasn't sure if someone had pushed him or not, the officer looked at me and asked, "Did you see anyone close to you or your brother near the time that this happened?"

"No," I answered.

"Did any of you see anyone or anything unusual on the boat?" he asked.

"Everybody was wearing a blue poncho," Chelsea said. "That was kind of unusual."

The officer just smiled at her and nodded his thanks. Then he asked Brandon if he had lost anything. He rustled around in his poncho for a minute and then said, "No. All I had was my wallet and it's still here."

He shook his wallet and started pulling things out to dry off.

"It's a good thing you weren't wearing flip-flops, like I am," I said. "You would have lost those for sure."

Brandon was wearing these really weird shoes with rubber soles and stretchy, thin tops that he had bought at a thrift store. "Yeah," he said, looking down at his feet. "They're almost dry already."

"Hey, Brandon," I laughed. "Maybe whoever pushed you was just trying to get you to lose those shoes."

He stared at them with a completely serious look and whispered, "Tragedy!"

The officers asked a few more questions, but since no one had seen anything, we didn't really have much to say.

"If you think of anything else," the officer said, "be sure to let us know."

When the police officers left, the boat captain escorted us to the gate.

"I apologize for the inconvenience," he said. Looking at Brandon, he asked, "Are you sure you're in good shape?"

"I'm fine," Brandon said.

"You know," smiled the officer, "if you would care for a swim, you might consider just checking into a hotel with a pool!"

"We already did!" said Danny with excitement. Then his face clouded over. "But we didn't get to go swimming yet."

We told the captain good-bye and left. As we were walking away we noticed a couple of employees emptying out large garbage cans that had "Poncho Recycling" printed on the sides of them.

"If you don't want your ponchos," one of them said to us, "we'll recycle them for you."

They continued to pull wads of blue plastic from the containers as we each tried to decide whether to keep our poncho or not. Chelsea and Danny both thought theirs were great and wanted to keep them, but I, for one, was more than happy to give mine up. It was getting hot again.

"Do you think I should keep mine?" Brandon asked. It seemed strange that he would ask. He usually didn't care what anybody else thought about the clothes that he wore—his shoes were an excellent example of that. I figured he was still slightly delirious from his fall into the river.

"You'll probably dry out faster without it," Dad suggested.

Mom added, "But we can go back to the hotel right now so you can change if you want."

"You don't want that thing," I said. "You look like a geek."

"Thanks, Jeff," Brandon mumbled.

"Besides," I said, "it has a rip in it." The hole in the poncho went right across one side of his chest. I stuck my hand through it and into his shirt pocket. "It makes it easy to get stuff in and out of your pocket, though!" I laughed.

Annoyed, Brandon pushed my arm away and then stopped short and grabbed his pocket through his poncho. "Oh, no!" he said.

He stood there holding his chest like a guy who was having a heart attack.

"Dad," Brandon finally said. "I think I lost the room key."

"Don't worry about it," Dad smiled. "It's probably halfway to Toronto by now. We'll get another one when we get back to the hotel."

"I'll pay for it," Brandon said.

"There's nothing to pay," Dad smiled. "That's why they use those magnetic cards; they're practically free. Besides that, they gave us two for each room. I still have the other one right here." He patted his back pocket as he spoke.

As we were giving our ponchos to one of the employees, the other one said, "Oh!" in disgust. "Don't people have a clue about the difference between garbage and recycling?"

"What did you find this time?" asked the first employee.

"A wig! Look at this!" As she spoke, she held up a wig of wet, long, brown hair.

CHAPTER 11

The Missing Letter

"Are you thinking what I'm thinking?" I asked Brandon.

"What?" he said back to me. He obviously was still a little affected by his fall into the river.

"Didn't you see that wig?" I asked.

"Yeah."

"Didn't it remind you of anything?" I asked, slightly annoyed that I had to spell it out for him.

"Yeah," Brandon nodded. "It looked like the dead muskrat that we saw washed up on the edge of the pond where Dad took us to feed the ducks when I was five. Remember that?"

I stared at him in total disbelief. "How about something in the last decade?" I said in disgust.

Brandon thought for a minute and then shook his head slowly. "Nope."

"The man who we've been seeing everywhere!" I practically yelled at him. "That wig looked just like his!"

"Oh, yeah," Brandon finally said. "It did, kind of."

His response was not nearly what I thought it should be. My fists that had been raised with intensity this whole time suddenly dropped to my sides in disappointment as I realized that Brandon just wasn't getting it.

"Never mind," I said, rolling my eyes. "We better catch up."

The rest of the family was about fifty feet in front of us, heading for the elevators. Brandon and I walked in silence for a few seconds before I tried to suggest to Brandon what I was thinking.

"What if that guy was on the boat, and he's the one that pushed you over the guardrail?" I suggested.

"I told you I don't know for sure if I was pushed or not," Brandon said.

"And what if he stole your room key from your pocket as he pushed you?" I asked.

"Oh, I can't imagine that anyone could have done that without me noticing," Brandon said. "Besides, Dad said the key was halfway to Toronto by now," Brandon said.

I just stared at him.

"Is that the way the river flows?" Brandon wondered out loud. "That means it's going north. I would have thought it went south—sort of like birds in the winter. Don't most rivers go south?"

I couldn't believe what I was hearing. "*What?*" I said. "Did you hit your head on a rock or something when you were in the river?" I asked. "When did you suddenly get calm and *bubble-brained?* When are you going to start freaking out like you always do?"

Brandon just stared at me like he had no idea what I was talking about. This was really strange. If Brandon no longer had the ability to be intense and out of control, then I knew that I was going to be lost. His extremeness in every situation was my anchor—my peace—my comfort. It was way too weird thinking that I might be paranoid about something more than Brandon was. I had to get help!

"Shauna!" I called.

Brandon and I had been walking quicker than everyone else and so we had almost caught up to them by this time. Shauna turned and waited for us.

"What?" she asked.

As calmly as I could, I asked her, "Did you see that wig that the girls found in the recycle bin?"

"Yeah," Shauna answered. Her eyebrows were raised, and I got the impression she had been thinking about it too.

"Did it remind you of anything?" I asked. She was about to answer, when I added, "And *don't* you dare bring up the dead muskrat from the bird pond ten years ago!"

"What?" she said with a confused look. "I wasn't! I was going to say that it looked like the hair on that guy who's been following us."

"Great," I said quietly.

"Do you think," Shauna paused before continuing, "that whoever pushed Brandon into the river maybe stole his room key at the same time?"

"Whew!" I breathed with relief. Suddenly all was right with the world again. I was not alone. It was a good feeling. "Yes-s-s," I hissed. "That's *exactly* what I told Brandon."

"The thought must be driving him crazy, huh?" Shauna laughed.

"No," I said soberly. "He doesn't get it."

Shauna's laugh stopped short and she stared at me in disbelief. She looked over her shoulder at Brandon who was walking a few feet behind us, apparently completely unaware of anything going on around him. We waited for him to catch up.

"Do you think the guy who's been following us stole your room key when he pushed you in the river?" Shauna asked. "And then he dumped his wig with the ponchos?"

"I don't see how," Brandon said flatly. "It doesn't seem reasonable, does it?"

"What about the letter?" I asked. "Don't you think that we should go back to the hotel room and make sure it's safe? Did Dad leave his notebook in our room or in the girls'?"

Brandon just brushed off the whole idea. "I'm sure it's fine," he said. "I don't want to go all the way back up there."

Shauna looked stunned by his response. "Okay," she nodded after a moment. Then she gave me a worried look and mouthed the words, "*Something's wrong!*"

I nodded my agreement. Brandon seemed totally unaware of our little exchange.

Mom and Dad had the elevator operator wait for the three of us to catch up before letting the doors close. After a couple seconds of silence, Dad asked Brandon, "How are you feeling?"

"I'm fine," Brandon smiled.

Shauna and I, who were standing slightly behind him, both stared at Dad and shook our heads.

"Should we go back to the hotel so you can change your clothes?" Mom asked.

"No," Brandon shook his head. "It's okay. I think I'll dry out pretty fast."

"Oh!" said the elevator operator with excitement. "Are you the kid who fell off the boat?"

Brandon nodded calmly. "That would be me."

"Wow," breathed the elevator guy. "That doesn't happen every day. Are you alright?"

"I'm fine," Brandon said again.

"Well, you act fine," smiled the operator.

Shauna and I stared at each other this time, again shaking our heads. After we got out of the elevator, we started walking up the sidewalk toward the busy part of the city. Dad hung back a little bit and pulled Shauna and me back with him.

"What was that all about?" Dad asked quietly. "Do you think something's wrong with Brandon?"

"Yeah," Shauna and I both said. Then I said, "We both told Brandon that maybe the guy with the long hair had stolen his room key, pushed him into the river, and then left that wig down there when he took off his poncho."

Shauna added, "We told him that maybe we better go check on the room and make sure the letter is safe." Then she asked, "Did you leave it your room or ours?"

Dad paused for a moment before answering. "It's in mine," he said. "But I agree with Brandon; I'm sure everything's fine."

"*Exactly!*" I said. "*You* agree with *Brandon!* When was the last time *that* happened?" I asked. "Something's wrong with either you or him—and since you're as *reasonable* as you always are—I'm betting it's *him!*"

"I see your point," Dad said quietly.

"I'm not going to be comfortable until he's back to his normal weird self," I said.

Shauna nodded her agreement. Dad didn't say anything else, but started walking quicker in order to catch up with the rest of the family. We stayed close behind. After catching up, Dad didn't say anything to anyone, but he kept glancing over at Brandon, watching him closely.

"What are we doing now?" Danny asked.

"I'm starving," Chelsea said.

"I know where I want to eat," Mom said. "It's a place just up ahead under the bridge. It's called The Secret Garden."

"Brandon," Meg said. "Weren't you in a play called *The Secret Garden?*"

"Huh?" he said. "Oh, yeah. But I don't want to eat right now. Can we go back to the hotel?"

"Sure," Dad said cautiously. "Is there something you want to check on?"

"I'm cold," Brandon said. "I just want to change my clothes."

Dad looked disappointed by his response. Shauna and I looked at each other with knowing looks.

The climb back up the three steep blocks seemed quite a bit harder than coming down. About halfway up I noticed that Brandon was suddenly in the lead. We were all struggling to keep up. When we got to the top and starting down the level street to our hotel, Brandon asked Dad, "Where did you put your blue notebook?"

"In our room," Dad answered cautiously again. "Why do you ask?"

"I was just starting to wonder if that B. Wright letter is safe," Brandon said slowly, "since I lost the room key."

Dad drew a deep, contented breath. He seemed to be happy that Brandon was finally showing signs of his normal self. I admit, the idea did my heart a bit of good as well.

"That's something to think about, all right," said Dad. "Let's go check it out." He started walking faster and Brandon stayed with him.

I didn't believe for a minute that Dad was worried about the letter, but personally, I was happy that we were going to check it out. The more I thought about it, the more worried I was beginning to get. Dad and Brandon practically ran the last half block to the hotel and through the lobby to the elevators. Shauna and I were right behind them, leaving the rest of the kids with Mom.

"Go!" Mom called to us when Shauna glanced back over her shoulder. "We'll catch up!"

When we got to the room and opened the door, Dad smiled and said, "Everything looks just the way we left it."

Brandon rushed past him and asked, "But where's the notebook?"

"It's right there on the table," Dad said. "You should find the letter at the very back."

Brandon quickly flipped open the book and then looked up. "It *should* be," he said, "but it's not. Are you sure this is where it was?"

Now Dad was the one to get a little frantic. He came over to the notebook and flipped a couple of pages back and forth. "It's gone, all right," he said finally. "I know it was here because I looked at it this morning right after we checked in. For some reason I had been thinking about it a lot on the drive over here." He looked up at us with sad eyes. "I was starting to wonder if we needed to be keeping it in a safer place—but I didn't do anything about it." He paused before adding, "I guess I should have followed my impression."

Just then a knock came at the door. It was Mom and everybody else.

"What are we doing now?" Mom asked.

"We're calling the police," Dad said. "The letter has been stolen."

Mom looked disappointed, but she didn't say anything.

A few minutes later we were down in the lobby of the hotel. While we were waiting for the police to get there, Dad asked the woman at the front desk to change the code on our door lock and to give us new access cards. She was happy to do it.

"Next time we lose an access card," Dad said, "I guess we should call ahead and have them change the code right then."

When the police came, we told them what had happened. They were the same two officers who had met us down at the dock. We also told them about the man who had been following us. Dad gave them both the Ohio license plate number and the New York plate number that we had seen behind the hotel earlier that morning. Apparently, Dad had thought to write it down before they all went up to the room. Sometimes, he doesn't do too badly.

One of the officers took the license plate numbers out to his car for a few minutes while the other officer asked us a few more questions. When the officer came back from the car he told us that both of the license plate numbers we had given him were stolen. Not the cars—just the license plates.

"The Ohio plates were reported missing last week," said the officer, "but the New York plates were reported just this morning."

"There are a lot of Ford Tauruses around," said the other officer.

"Yeah," I said, "but this one is a putrid green color."

"I have that down," said the officer, glancing at his clipboard.

"Did you use the word *putrid*?" I asked.

"No," the officer said without a smile. "I just wrote *green*. That will be sufficient."

Once the police were gone, Dad said he wanted to go up to the room to call the FBI. "Is that all right with you, Jeff?" he asked.

"Yeah," I said. "Now that I know it hasn't been Agent Smith who was following us."

"I'll just be a minute," Dad said. The rest of us stayed in the lobby until he returned about five minutes later.

"What did they say?" I asked.

"They are off the case," Dad said.

"Wait, what?" said Shauna.

"Why?" asked Brandon.

"Because their missing person is no longer missing," Dad explained.

"But what about the document?" I asked.

"That's not missing anymore, either," Dad said. He shook his head like he wasn't sure he understood the whole thing. I had to agree. "It turns out," Dad continued, "that the missing man was really simply on vacation. Apparently, his supervisor had mistakenly thought the guy's vacation was the first two weeks of *next* month—not *this* month."

"No way!" I said in disbelief.

"How dopey!" agreed Brandon with one side of his nose screwed up.

"But what about the document?" Shauna asked. "Wasn't it missing?"

Dad shook his head like he couldn't believe what he had heard. "I guess before this guy went on vacation, he just didn't put it back where it was supposed to go. He apparently had it in a certain place in his desk because he had been working on it."

"If the FBI really thought he was missing," Mom said, "wouldn't they have searched his desk?"

"That's what I asked," nodded Dad. "They did search it, but since the guy knew he wasn't supposed to be keeping documents in his desk, he had a sort of hiding place for it that the searches missed."

"Wait a minute," I stammered. "So you're saying that neither the guy nor the document were *ever missing* and so the FBI is just done with the whole thing? But what about the guy who's been following us? He had a copy of the document. And what about our letter that was stolen?"

Dad drew a deep breath. "We have no proof that anyone has been following us," he said. "And it's not illegal for someone to have a copy of that document."

"But how did he get it?" Brandon burst out.

"I asked the agent about that," Dad said. "The missing man—who's not missing—told them that he gave a copy to some historian a month or so ago, along with some copies of some other documents. Apparently, they do it fairly often."

"What?" Brandon asked.

Dad held up his hands and said, "There's no evidence that anything illegal has happened."

"What about the stolen letter?" I said again.

"We're in *Canada*," Dad answered. "The FBI has nothing to do with things that happen outside the United States, unless there's some sort of connection."

"But there *is!*" Brandon said.

"Not that *they* can see," Dad explained. "So there's not much we can do about it at this point."

We all grumbled a little more, but the conversation was basically done. I couldn't believe it. Was it really that hard to piece the whole thing together? It took a while, but I finally managed to quit being so bugged by the whole thing. It helped that we left and started doing some other things.

Mom still wanted to go the restaurant that was under the bridge by the river. It turned out to be pretty cool. We had a long table right next to the windows, so we had a perfect view of Niagara Falls as we ate. The best part about it, though, was that Brandon seemed to be back to his normal self. He was joking and laughing right along with the rest of us. But every few minutes his face would cloud over and he would say something about the missing letter again.

"What if the guy who stole the letter gets the treasure before we get back?" Brandon asked once.

"Marion is supposed to be an expert on this," Dad said, "and it's taking him almost a week to get it figured out. It doesn't seem too likely that anyone else could do it before tomorrow when we get back."

"Besides," Mom said. "The letter is absolutely no good unless they know exactly what house we're talking about, right?" She smiled and said, "I don't think we have much to worry about."

"Much?" Brandon asked.

"I'm sure things will work out fine," Dad said. "They always do."

Brandon acted like he didn't totally agree with them, but he seemed resigned to make the best of it. He didn't bring it up again for the rest of the evening.

Dinner was great and Mom had a few more things on her "must see" list, but we were all tired and agreed to just go back to the hotel. We did make a quick stop at the Hershey's store again—just long enough to buy a year's supply of fudge. Mom and Dad bought some of each person's favorite. We were careful to each choose a different favorite from everyone else so that we could walk out of there with as much fudge as possible.

"Can we go swimming now?" Danny asked as we entered the hotel lobby and our noses caught the whiff of chlorine. "The pool's inside," he beamed at Dad.

Dad hesitated for a minute before answering, "Sure. I'll go swimming with you and anyone else can come who wants to."

"Yippee!" Danny said.

We all ended up at the pool. Mom and Meg brought books

instead of swimming suits, though. That meant the rest of us had to be careful not to splash in their direction.

At one point Brandon said, "Swimming is a lot easier in a swimsuit, instead of being completely dressed and covered in a poncho." We all laughed.

The next morning Dad woke us up three times before I bothered to do anything about getting up.

"Breakfast ends in an hour!" Dad said the first time. "Better get up now if you're going to shower first."

"I'm not," I mumbled into my pillow.

I thought I heard Brandon say, "Me either."

Danny, of course, launched himself out of bed as soon as he heard the word *breakfast*. He stopped short, though, when he heard the rest of Dad's comment and asked, "Do I have to shower first?"

"No," I heard Dad say. "You had a bath last night after swimming, didn't you?"

"Oh, yeah!" Danny said.

A moment later I heard the door close. The next thing I remember is Dad saying, "Breakfast ends in half an hour! Better get up now if you want some. You might even still have time for a quick shower."

"No, thanks," I mumbled.

Brandon mumbled something, too, but I couldn't tell what it was.

I heard Danny say, "Can I go back and have another one of those little muffins?"

"Let's go," Dad said, and I heard the door close again.

The next thing I remember is Dad saying, "Breakfast ends in fifteen minutes!"

Before I said anything I caught a whiff of something that smelled really good.

"Who brought food up here?" Brandon mumbled, sitting up.

"I did," Dad said with pleasure, "in an effort to get you guys moving."

It worked. Brandon and I each pulled on some clothes and headed to the lobby. Mom and all the girls were already down there. There were a whole bunch of other people down there, too. And all of them looked like senior citizens—or at least pretty close to it.

I looked at Dad and said, "Is Niagara Falls just for grandparents?"

"No!" Dad laughed.

"Is that why no one else was swimming last night when we were here?" I asked.

"No," Dad said again. "Lots of families come here."

"I don't remember seeing any other kids besides Chelsea and Danny walking around town last night wearing midget ponchos," Brandon said, joining the conversation.

"I saw plenty of them," Dad said. "You just weren't looking."

"Hey, Dad!" Shauna called from one of the tables. She was standing next to a table of four or five people. One looked about Dad's age, but the rest looked quite a bit older. And they all had name tags. "Dad, come here," Shauna said as she motioned for him to come over. Brandon and I followed. Danny was already back at the buffet table getting another mini-muffin.

"This is Brother Applewood, my religion professor from last year," Shauna said. "This is my dad, Craig Andrews."

They shook hands and both said how nice it was to meet the other one.

"What brings you here, Brother Applewood?" Dad asked.

"All of these people," Brother Applewood smiled with a wave of his arm. "Those with name tags, anyway," he smiled.

"Brother Applewood is the tour director for a Church history tour," Shauna explained.

"Really?" said Dad. "That sounds fun."

Mom had joined us by this time. She asked, "Where have you been and where are you are going?"

"And what is my purpose here on earth?" Brother Applewood asked with a laugh. Then he said, "Sorry, it was starting to sound a lot like a missionary discussion about the plan of salvation!"

"They're going to Kirtland today," Shauna said.

"That's right," said Brother Applewood. "We started in Boston and have seen sites in Vermont, Pennsylvania, and New York. We're heading all the way to Nauvoo before we fly home."

"Sounds great," Dad said. "We're just hitting sites near Kirtland and Palmyra. We're heading back to Kirtland today, just like you. Then we'll fly out of Cleveland in a couple of days."

"Oh, it's too bad you're not making it any farther east," said Brother Applewood. "There are some great things to see back there."

"That would have been fun," agreed Dad.

"If I had time," said Brother Applewood, "I would just love to tell you about it."

"Oh, you're very kind!" said Mom. "Maybe next trip."

"Hey," said Brother Applewood suddenly, snapping his fingers. "Why don't some of you ride with us on the bus? There's plenty of room. Then I could tell you all about the places we've already seen."

Shauna said, "That would be so fun!" Turning to Mom and Dad, she asked, "May I?"

"Uh-h, I don't see why not," Dad said. Then he asked, "But will the bus company allow it?"

Brother Applewood smiled and said, "We often invite a local tour guide to ride on the bus with us for a few hours at a time. They simply sign an insurance waiver form, and we're good to go. The form even allows for minor children as long as the form is signed by their legal guardian."

"It's okay with me," Mom agreed. "We can just follow behind you in the van."

"Great!" said Brother Applewood. "I think this could really work out well. We'll be riding for several hours, during which I really won't be presenting any information to the group. They will mostly have all the time to themselves, so we'll have lots of time to talk about what they have already seen." Looking at Brandon and me he said, "Would you two like to come with us?"

"Sure," Brandon said. "Riding in a bus for a while might make our van seem small again."

Brother Applewood laughed.

"I'll go, too," I said.

We agreed to meet outside the front of the hotel in about an hour. When Meg heard what we were doing, she didn't want to be left out. So Dad decided that the four of us would ride in the bus, and Mom and Dad would follow in the van with Chelsea and Danny. Shauna kept talking about how great Brother Applewood is and how much he knew about everything and how much fun it was going to be to ride with him for a while. Personally, I just figured that if Dad had someone he was supposed to keep up with, then he wouldn't be taking any spontaneous detours along the way. Chloe and Rudy were expecting us that afternoon, and Marion said he would have the information ready. I just wanted to get there as soon as we could. I mentioned my logic to Brandon and he agreed. It was nice to have him back to normal.

CHAPTER 12

The Wheels on the Bus

Our temporary adoption into the Church History tour group began with the four of us getting name tags. Most of the people on the tour went out of their way to introduce themselves to "the new group members" for a minute or two before finding their own table where they would finish their breakfast. It was really interesting to watch how Shauna, Meg, and Brandon each interacted with them. Shauna was always very polite and complimentary. Meg was giggly and tried very hard to answer questions either by shaking her head or using a single word. Brandon seemed the most comfortable of all, however. He wasn't afraid to ask them questions about themselves that I never would have. And from the look on Shauna's face, I got the impression she agreed with me.

At one point a man came up and shook hands with each of us. He was returning from the buffet table with a small plate of waffles covered in fresh strawberries and whipped cream. *Amos* was written across his name tag. We spoke for a minute or so and then his wife came up and introduced herself. Her name was Lynnette. She looked at the plate Amos was holding and said, "You told me you were going after strawberries, Amos. I sure hope you don't think I'm going to stand by and let you eat all that other stuff, too."

Turning to us, she said, "The doctor put him on a special diet, and he knows he can't have all that." She heaved a sigh and said,

"But he just ignores it! He's an ignoramus!" Looking at Meg, Lynnette asked, "Do you know what an ignoramus is, young lady?"

Meg nodded, obviously hoping that would be sufficient. But when the lady waited patiently for more of an answer, Meg said quietly, "It's a person who's ignorant or very foolish."

"Exactly," said Lynnette. "You're a smart girl."

I stared at Meg in amazement, wondering what kind of books taught her words like that.

Lynnette looked at her husband and said, "And when you ignore what the doctor tells you, Amos, that's when you're an ignoramus!"

"I wasn't going to eat it," Amos defended himself. "But the strawberries just look a lot tastier like this, don't you think?"

Lynnette just smiled and excused herself.

After she was gone Brandon said, "Tell me, Amos, would you have eaten all that if she hadn't caught you—or were you just checking to she if she still cares?"

"You can see right through me, son," Amos winked.

"I thought so," Brandon smiled.

"I just eat my strawberry waffles without the waffles," Amos smiled. "If you want to see something unusual," Amos said, leaning in closer as if he were sharing a big secret with us, "you ought to see the way she makes herself a banana split—she does it with every-thing except ice cream! She doesn't like ice cream!"

"Really?" we all said at once.

Amos nodded and said, walking away to join his wife, "I call it her Anti-Nephi-Sundae."

Over the next few minutes I glanced several times at the table where Amos was sitting. He carefully ate every last one of the strawberries, leaving the whipped cream and waffles behind.

"I like these people," Brandon said during a small break in intro-ductions. "They each have their own style and don't seem to care what anyone else thinks." He smiled and gestured with his head toward a man who was standing at the buffet table. "Check out the socks on that guy, for instance," Brandon said.

I hadn't noticed before, but the man was wearing white athletic socks with sandals, and the socks stuck straight out at least two inches beyond the front of his sandals. "Now that's style," Brandon smiled.

When the man came to our table a few minutes later we found out his name was David. And true to form, Brandon asked him about his socks. "I wear them this way," David explained, "because every lamebrain in this hemisphere who makes socks always puts the seam right along the end of the toes—and it's irritating! I inherited sensitive toes from my grandmother on my father's side. So I buy them big enough that I can leave them just hanging out the front."

"Sounds like a great plan," I said.

"I even tried these new athletic socks for this trip," David went on. "I figured athletes would have comfortable socks—but they're no better!"

Most of the group members didn't bother to share their doctor's advice or their frustrations over socks, but all of them were very nice and most of them were quite funny. When breakfast was over we headed back to our room to pack. Dad made sure that we were all ready and out in front of the hotel at the agreed on time. Most of the tour group was there, too, but there were a few stragglers.

"Where should we meet in case we get separated?" Dad asked Brother Applewood. No one else I know would have thought to ask that question. They agreed to meet at the tour group's hotel in Kirtland, so Dad got out his blue binder and wrote down the address.

"Don't you think we'll just be able to stay together?" Brandon asked.

As Dad closed his binder and pushed the cap back on his pen, he said, "Brandon, I like to prepare for the worst, but hope for the best."

"Thanks, Dad," Brandon said. "I think I'll hire someone to embroider that on a pillow and I'll give it to you for Christmas."

"Cathy is good with things like that," I offered, referring to a friend of ours from school.

Brother Applewood sat in the seat right behind the bus driver and he gave us the front two rows across the aisle. He put us there so that he could tell us everything that we had missed from the first part of their tour. As always, Meg had her pink backpack with her, and Shauna brought along her laptop computer. I figured she was thinking she might want to watch a movie if things got too boring on the bus. Brandon and I didn't bring anything with us. We had backpacks in the van, of course, but we figured we could live without them for a few hours.

We all smiled at Amos and Lynnette as they climbed onto the bus. Pointing to the seat behind Brother Applewood, Amos said, "I believe this is where we sit today."

Lynnette sat next to the window and Amos fell backwards into the aisle seat across from me. He looked over at us and said, "Everybody is supposed to change seats by moving one bench each day in a counter-clockwise rotation around the bus. Normally we would have been sitting where you are, but all of us in the front agreed to move a couple of extra benches today in order to make room for you kids."

"Oh, you're very kind!" said Shauna from the front bench. "We didn't mean to get in your way."

"No worries!" said Amos with a wink. "We are used to making adjustments. There are half a dozen folks on the bus who sit in the same seat every day, no matter what—especially those in the back."

"It's like that on our school bus, too," Brandon said.

Once everyone had boarded the bus and the doors were closed,

Brother Applewood stood and asked Amos, "Will you offer our opening prayer today, Amos?"

"I've been planning on it," Amos nodded. He turned to me and whispered, "The bench behind the director is always responsible for the prayers that day."

Brother Applewood took the microphone from the bus driver and announced, "I believe most—if not all—of you are aware that we have some guests with us today. Shauna was a religion student of mine this past year at BYU. She is joined by her younger brothers Jeff and Brandon, and her younger sister Meg." I was impressed that he got all of our names right without looking at our name tags. Brother Applewood continued by saying, "I thought we would give Meg, the youngest, the opportunity to select our opening song today." With that, he looked over at Meg and smiled.

"Me?" Meg asked with big eyes. "You want me to pick a song?"

"What's your favorite hymn or Primary song?" Brother Applewood asked her.

Meg thought for a moment and then said, "I Love to See the Temple." The way she said it sounded like a question. She looked up at Brother Applewood like she was afraid she had given the wrong answer.

Brother Applewood announced the song and prayer. A woman named Macie with short, dark hair came up and led the song. She smiled into the microphone, "I've been a chorister in Primary for years, so I know this song." And she did, too. She sang every word perfectly.

After Amos said the prayer, the bus headed down the street and across the bridge. Brother Applewood suggested into the microphone that everyone take one last look at Niagara Falls.

"And look!" I said, pointing at the river. "There's Brandon's swimming pool!"

Once we were across the bridge Brother Applewood announced that David would be giving the devotional. David came to the front, passing out a sheet of paper to everyone along the way. Then he sat next to Brother Applewood, holding the microphone. I smiled at his socks. His devotional was about the importance of doing temple work for our ancestors.

David said into the microphone, "I want to read you some of the words of Joseph Smith the Prophet, which are found in Section 128 of the Doctrine and Covenants."

My first thought was that Dad would be pleased that David said *Doctrine and Covenants* and didn't just use the abbreviation *D&C*.

"What I'm going to be reading to you is taken from verses eighteen through twenty-four," David said.

As he read, I followed along on the paper he had given each of us.

David read, "'It is sufficient to know . . . that the earth will be smitten with a curse unless there is a welding link of some kind or other between the fathers and the children.'"

Turning to Meg, David asked, "Do you know what welding is?"

"Uh-huh," said Meg. "That's when two things are joined together and can't be broken apart."

"I couldn't have said it better myself," smiled David. He held the microphone over close to Meg and had her repeat her definition of welding. I just shook my head in amazement.

David continued reading, "'. . . there is a welding link of some kind or other between the fathers and the children, upon some subject or other—and behold what is that subject?'"

I don't think David intended for anyone to answer the question, but Brandon was getting into the spirit of things and blurted out, "Baptism for the dead!"

David looked a little surprised, but also pleased. He continued by reading, "'It is the baptism for the dead. For we without them cannot be made perfect; neither can they without us be made perfect. Neither can they nor we be made perfect without those who have died in the gospel also; for it is necessary in the ushering in of the dispensation of the fulness of times, which dispensation is now beginning to usher in, that a whole and complete and perfect union, and welding together of dispensations, and keys, and powers, and glories should take place, and be revealed from the days of Adam even to the present time.'"

David stopped reading and said, "That means we all need to be linked in a chain all the way back to Adam. We all have forefathers that are waiting for us to find them and link ourselves to them. Now in verse twenty-two we read that we can 'redeem them out of their prison; for the prisoners shall go free.'"

David paused for a moment and then said, "I won't read it all, but Joseph Smith gave us a charge in verse twenty-four that we 'offer unto the Lord an offering in righteousness.' We read, 'Let us, therefore, as a church and a people, and as Latter-day Saints, offer unto the Lord an offering in righteousness; and let us present in his holy temple, when it is finished, a book containing the records of our dead, which shall be worthy of all acceptation.'"

After he finished reading from the paper, David bore his testimony about the importance of doing temple work for our dead forefathers. He said they are depending on us and waiting on us. It made me think about the discussions our family had had about Elijah and the sealing power.

Still seated because the bus was moving, Brother Applewood used the microphone to thank David for the devotional. Then he said, "According to my notes, no one has a birthday today. It's been several days since we've sung happy birthday to anyone. I propose that we sing happy birthday to the young lady who picked our opening song."

I heard Meg say, "But my birthday's not until December fourteenth!"

"That's close enough!" smiled Brother Applewood. "We're more than halfway there."

After the birthday song Brother Applewood gave the

microphone back to the driver. He said to the four of us, "I guess I should have warned you about how we start out each day."

"That's fine," Shauna said. "It's pretty much the same as our family does."

Brandon added, "Only our family's devotionals are usually longer."

"And we don't sing happy birthday to people who aren't having a birthday," Meg said.

At this point Brother Applewood began telling us about the first few days of their tour. It was really pretty interesting. For at least an hour, he kept pulling out small maps and brochures to show us all sorts of things. I think we all enjoyed it.

When he was done he asked if we wanted to know about Missouri and Nauvoo, too, but we told him that our family had been to those places three years earlier.

"I'll bet that was fun," Brother Applewood smiled. "Are there any favorite places that you can remember?"

"My favorite place was Adam-ondi-Ahman," I said.

"That's just because we were run off the road by some crazy guy in a cool-looking truck that you wanted," Brandon said. "Then we were stuck in the mud for hours until someone could tow us out!"

"I *still* want a bright red, Dodge four-wheel drive with a roll bar and lights across the top," I said. "But that's *not* why I liked Adam-ondi-Ahman."

"Why did you like it?" asked Brother Applewood.

"Because of what happened there," I said. "It is so amazing to think that Adam gathered all of his posterity there and talked to them and blessed them! There were hundreds of generations there at the same time. We don't have that anymore."

"I know," Shauna agreed. "Most of us are lucky to know our grandparents, and a few might know a great-grandparent. Sometimes when I look at Danny I think about how he will never really remember Granny." Turning to Brother Applewood, Shauna explained, "Our mom's mom lived with us until she died of cancer. Our little brother, Daniel, was only four or five at the time."

Brother Applewood nodded his understanding.

"I know," Brandon agreed. "Mom and Dad have been doing family history for years and they are still stuck on our triple great-grandfather. No one can figure out who his parents are or where he came from."

"After all that work," smiled Brother Applewood, "what a treasure it will be when his parents are found."

"If we all still lived as long as Adam did," I said, "that wouldn't be a problem."

"You're right," Brandon nodded.

For the next while Brandon and I talked about what we were going to do once we got back to Kirtland. We were both pretty anxious to find out what Marion had figured out so we could get over to Rudy and Chloe's house to see what we could find. We also spent a while making guesses about the guy who had been following us, but we never could come up with anything that made sense.

Meanwhile, Shauna and Brother Applewood spent the time talking about the religion class she had taken from him. His name tag had his first name written on it, but since Shauna kept calling him "Brother Applewood," so did I. I think Meg was pleased to be able to use the time to read from one of the huge books she was toting around in her pink backpack.

A while later Macie, the Primary chorister, came back to the front of the bus and asked Brother Applewood if she could lead the group in a song. She took the microphone and said, "It's so nice to have some younger people with us today, I was thinking we ought to try to make them feel a little more comfortable. So we're going to sing 'The Wheels on the Bus.' How many of you remember that song?" Without waiting for an answer, she said, "We used to always sing that song on the way home from school when I was little."

"You're still little!" came a call from a man somewhere behind us.

"When I was young!" said Macie into the microphone.

Then she immediately launched into the song, singing, "The wheels on the bus go round and round, round and round, round and round," and so on. After the verse ended she asked for people to suggest other verses that they knew. We must have sung at least ten different verses, most of which I'd never heard of before.

We sang that "the wipers on the bus go swish, swish, swish," followed by "the babies on the bus go wah, wah, wah."

When we finished with that one, Amos said, "That's why we don't invite babies!"

Then we sang "the mommies on the bus go shh, shh, shh." There were verses for grandmas and grandpas and almost everything else you can think of. After we sang "the drivers on the bus say 'Move on back'," our bus driver came up with his own version. He pointed to Macie and said, "The drivers on the bus say 'Sit down now!'" Macie immediately sat on the bench next to Brother Applewood and led us all in that verse.

All in all, it was a very eventful bus ride. There were two other things I enjoyed about the ride: the fact that there were no seat belts, and the people who brought snacks and candy shared with everyone. They brought a lot better stuff than what Mom and Dad allowed in our van.

It was late afternoon when we arrived at the tour group's hotel in Kirtland. Mom and Dad were not behind us. The bus had made one rest stop on the way from Niagara Falls, and they had been with us then, but no one had any idea how long it had been since they were right behind us.

"It's a good thing Dad wrote down the address," Shauna said.

"Call Cathy!" I said. "Get her working on that embroidered pillow as soon as possible!"

Brandon laughed.

Brother Applewood went inside to help the tour group get checked in. He came out a few minutes later and said, "Your parents called and left a message for us at the front desk."

"Where are they?" Shauna asked.

"Well, apparently," Brother Applewood explained, "they pulled off to go see a Church history site in Pennsylvania, but their van got stuck in the mud. As soon as they get someone to pull them out, they will be on their way again."

"Je-e-eff!" Brandon said. "It's all *your* fault!"

"What?" I said.

"You brought up Adam-ondi-Ahman," Brandon explained. "They were cursed by the memory of getting stuck."

"Right," I smirked.

"The note says that they'll be here as soon as they can," said Brother Applewood, "and we should call your mother's mobile phone to tell them where they can find the four of you."

"Where would we go?" Meg asked.

"You're welcome to come with us," said Brother Applewood. "After we get checked in, we'll be visiting some of the sites in Kirtland."

That didn't sound too great to me. We had already seen everything just a few days earlier.

I think Brandon was thinking the same thing I was when he said, "Well, there are some people who were expecting us to visit them this afternoon. Maybe we can just go over there."

"Oh, that's right," Shauna said. "We told Chloe and Rudy that we would be back today."

"Who are Chloe and Rudy?" asked Brother Applewood.

"They're people who live in the same house that our triple great-grandfather lived in," Shauna said. "In the early 1830s."

"Wow!" said Brother Applewood. "It's the original house?"

"Yes," nodded Shauna.

"Well, maybe we can just take you over there on our way to the visitors' center," suggested Brother Applewood. "That would be a site to see."

"Sounds great!" we all agreed.

Brother Applewood left us in the lobby and went to help the group finish checking in.

"Do you think we can get the bus to stop at the library on the way?" Brandon asked.

"Oh, yeah," I said. "We need to see what Marion was able to figure out."

Shauna thought for a moment and then glanced quickly around the room. She pointed to a phone that was sitting on an end table in the corner of the lobby. "Maybe we can just call him," she said.

"Do you think it's okay if we use this phone?" Meg asked, as we walked over to the table.

There was a phonebook under the table and a sign next to the phone that read, "Dial 9 for Outside Line."

"I'm sure it is," Shauna said. "See the sign?"

Using the phonebook, Shauna looked up the number for the Kirtland Public Library. "May I speak to Marion, please?" she said into the phone, followed by, "Thank you, I'll wait." She waited for almost a full minute before it looked like someone was talking to her again.

"Oh, he did?" Shauna said. "So will he be back tomorrow?" Pause. "Thank you," she said and hung up the phone. Looking at us now, she screwed up her face and said, "We just missed him."

"Do you think we can call him at home?" Brandon asked.

"Don't you remember Dad saying that they wouldn't give us his home number?" I asked.

"Maybe we can find it in the phonebook," Brandon suggested.

"We don't know his last name," Shauna said.

After more discussion, the best thing we could come up with was that maybe Chloe and Rudy would know how to get hold of him and hopefully we would be able to talk them into it before Dad got here and squashed the whole thing.

As soon as the tour group was checked in, we all loaded on the bus again and headed for Chloe and Rudy's house. Rudy must have heard the bus rumbling down his normally quiet street because he came out to see what was going on. Brother Applewood followed the four of us off the bus to go talk to Rudy. Meg was wearing her backpack and Shauna was carrying the computer bag.

"You made it back!" said Rudy.

"Yep," Shauna said.

"But where are your parents?" Rudy asked.

"They had car trouble," said Brother Applewood. "We were driving to Kirtland in tandem this afternoon, but they ended up getting delayed."

Rudy and Brother Applewood introduced themselves to each other and exchanged greetings.

"The children said that you were planning on them visiting you this afternoon," said Brother Applewood. "Is that correct?"

"Been lookin' forward to it all week," smiled Rudy. He put his thumbs into the sides of his belt and looked at us. "So does that mean that me and the Missus get to entertain you this evening until your parents arrive?"

"If that's alright," Shauna said. "We don't want to be in your way."

"Balderdash," scoffed Rudy. "We couldn't think of anything we'd like better. C'mon inside. Have you had supper?"

"No!" said Brandon, seizing the opportunity. This was the first time I realized that I was hungry, too.

"Great," said Brother Applewood. "We'll be on our way then. It was nice having you along!"

We all thanked him and shook his hand. He smiled when Shauna told him that she was going to try to take another religion class from him.

When we went inside the house, Chloe seemed just as happy to see us as Rudy had.

"They haven't had supper yet," Rudy told Chloe.

"Well, put them up to the table then," Chloe said to Rudy. Turning to Shauna and Meg, Chloe said, "You two can just put your bags down there in the corner. I'll make some sandwiches. Then the rest of your family can sit down as soon as they arrive."

"Are you sure? We don't want to cause a lot of work," Shauna said.

"Oh, don't be silly," Chloe said. "It's no trouble at all."

"May I use your phone to tell our parents where we are?" Shauna asked.

"Of course," said Rudy. "Use the phone in the parlor," he added, pointing.

Shauna made the call and then returned to the kitchen. "They said they'll pick us up here in a couple of hours."

As Chloe was handing Rudy a stack of plates to carry to the table, he asked her, "Do you think we should wait for the parents of these young 'uns to get here before we tell them that someone was prowling around last night and dug a big hole out in the side yard?"

CHAPTER 13

The Treasure Hunters

The four of us froze where we were and stared at Rudy. Chloe was staring at him, too.

"Sounds to me," Chloe said, "like you've already answered that question. If you wanted to tell them, why did you bother to ask me?"

"You know I like getting your dander up whenever I can," chuckled Rudy. He put the stack of plates on the table and said, "Come out in the yard and let me show you something."

We followed Rudy out the back of his house and around to the side where there was a large yard. Not far from the house the ground began to slope gradually up a hill until it was at least as high as the roof of the house. Thick trees covered the top. Not far from the top of the hill was a large hole. As we walked closer to it I saw that the hole was about five feet across and almost that deep. The pile of dirt next to the hole was dark and moist, without a rock in sight.

"A hole that size in Utah," I said, "would turn up about a thousand rocks."

"Don't get too many rocks around here," said Rudy. "Except down close to the river."

"You said someone dug this last night?" Shauna asked. "And you don't know who it was?"

"That's right," said Rudy, with his thumbs hooked on his belt again.

Brandon got a scared look on his face and said, "I wonder if it was the same guy who stole the letter!"

We all stared silently at Brandon for a moment before Rudy asked, "You talking about the letter you got from us?"

"That's right," Shauna nodded.

"It got stolen?" Rudy asked.

"Right out of our hotel room in Niagara Falls," I said. "And whoever it was didn't take anything else. They knew what they wanted."

"Did you see anybody?" Brandon asked Rudy, trying to find some reason for hope.

"Nope," said Rudy, "but heard some sounds."

We waited for him to continue. "Just after dark last night," Rudy said, "me and the Missus were heading for bed when I heard some loud cracking sounds followed by a huge thud in the yard on the other side of the house. I went to see what had happened, but when I got there all I found was a broken tree limb on the ground."

"Did you call the police?" Brandon asked again.

"Sure didn't," Rudy said. "I was out in the yard for a few minutes sniffing around, but I never saw or heard anything else, so I came back inside and headed for bed. I just reckoned the limb had broken off by itself and fallen to the ground."

"So when did you find this hole?" Shauna asked.

"Just before dawn this morning," answered Rudy. "I heard some noises out here and came out to see what was going on. But this spot is so far from the house that the porch light didn't reach up here well enough to see much. As soon as I came out, though, I heard what sounded like a couple of people scampering into the trees."

"Did you call the police?" Brandon asked again.

"Not directly," said Rudy. "First I came up here to see what I could see. When I found this hole, then I went back inside the house and phoned the police."

"Did they catch the guys?" Brandon asked.

"Naw," said Rudy. "I'm sure they were already long gone by then. They probably took off as soon as I was back in the house. But the sun was up by the time the police arrived, and they discovered some interesting things."

"Like what?" I asked.

"Like the broken tree limb on the other side of the house," Rudy said. "It wasn't big enough by itself to make a thud as loud as the one I heard."

"Really?" I said.

"And there was fresh mud on top of the broken limb," Rudy continued. "The police say it looked like someone had been standing on it. I figured the branch must have broken out from under him, and the thud I heard was a *man* hitting the ground—not just a tree limb."

"That's the east side of the house, isn't it?" Shauna asked.

"That's correct, young lady," Rudy nodded. "And the police discovered something else interesting. While one of them was here lookin' over this hole, another one borrowed my ladder and climbed up to get a better look at the tree where the limb broke off." Rudy paused for a moment and then said slowly, "You'll never guess what the man in the tree saw."

He had just said that we would never guess it, but then he just stood there waiting, like he expected us to try!

"What?" Meg breathed. I had completely forgotten that she was even there with us, but the look on her face told me that she was not only there, she was completely caught up in what Rudy was saying.

Rudy looked at Meg and said, "This hole."

"What?" Brandon asked. He looked like he was as confused as I was.

"From the tree on the other side of the house," Rudy explained, "he was able to look straight through the windows on both sides of the house and see this here hole." Rudy pointed dramatically at the large opening as he said the last word.

"Oh, no!" Brandon moaned. "That means that the guy who stole the letter used it to find this spot and steal the money!"

"Wait, what?" Shauna said.

"Don't you get it?" Brandon asked. "The guy read the letter and figured out where the sun comes up, looked through the window and saw this spot! That's why they dug the hole here."

"But I don't think they found anything," said Rudy.

Brandon stopped short in the middle of a moan and asked, "What makes you so sure?"

"Because I scared them away," explained Rudy. "If they had found something they would have already left."

A smile crept slowly across Brandon's face—and mine too, for that matter.

"Oh, yeah!" Brandon said with excitement. "So did you dig anymore after they were gone?" he asked. "To see if you could find anything?"

"Didn't figure on wasting my time," said Rudy, "until Marion tells us if they were even in the right spot."

Brandon's face fell again.

"We called the library a while ago," said Shauna, "but Marion had already gone home for the day. They said to call back tomorrow."

"Do you think he would mind if we called him at home?" I asked.

"And do you have his phone number?" Brandon asked, looking a little hopeful again.

"I don't reckon he would mind at all," smiled Rudy, starting back toward the house. "Let's go give him a ring, shall we?"

We all excitedly followed Rudy across the lawn and inside the house. When we got inside the kitchen, we found that Chloe had a large plate of sandwiches waiting for us. These sandwiches were like nothing I had ever tasted before in my life. If there is such a thing as a gourmet bologna sandwich, that's what these were. They were piled so thick that I was sure I was going to have trouble opening my mouth wide enough to take a bite. I don't think I could make a complete list of everything she put on those sandwiches if I tried. Partly because there were some things on there that I'm sure I've never heard of—and I wasn't feeling up to asking what they were, either.

While Rudy went into the parlor to call Marion, Chloe invited us to say grace over the sandwiches and dig in. Shauna offered the prayer and we all started to eat. Meg was having trouble getting her small hands around her sandwich, let alone getting the thing into her mouth. Chloe showed her how to go at it on an angle and soon Meg was chomping away like the rest of us.

When Rudy came back into the kitchen he said, "Marion's coming over a little later."

"Does he have it figured out?" I asked, as soon as I had swallowed enough that I thought I could be polite about it.

"He does indeed," Rudy said, sitting down at the kitchen table with us. He picked up a sandwich and took a large bite. We all watched as Rudy closed his eyes and chewed very slowly and carefully. He seemed to be loving every bite.

"No woman in the world," Rudy said after finally swallowing the rest of his first bite, "makes a bologna sandwich like this." He looked over at Chloe and added, "And just think—I married her before I'd ever had one of these!" He smiled and took another large bite, savoring it as much as the first.

"Did Rudy tell you kids that someone else was here asking questions about you?" Chloe asked us.

We all froze at the thought. "No," Shauna finally answered. "Who was it?"

"He said he was an FBI agent," said Chloe. "He said his name was Agent Smith."

"Ha!" I said. "I was right all along."

"What questions did he ask about us?" Shauna asked.

Chloe looked over at me and said, "He wanted to know if you had told us anything about an old document."

"We told him we didn't remember anything like that," Rudy interjected.

Rudy took another bite of his sandwich, so Chloe continued by saying, "He told us that you had a message that spoke of a treasure hidden in this home by the man who lived here in the early 1830s. We told him that we didn't remember for sure. But after he had gone, I seemed to remember that when we first read that letter from behind the baseboard, that you kids said something about it being like a note that someone had. Am I remembering correctly?" Chloe looked at Brandon.

Shauna turned to Meg and asked, "Do you still have it?"

Meg asked, "Do you mean my bookmark?"

"Yes," said Shauna.

Meg reached into her backpack and pulled out the slip of paper that had the message she got from the man on the phone. She handed it to Chloe, who read it silently and then handed it to Rudy. He read it to himself and handed it back to Meg.

"By itself," Chloe said, "it doesn't give a lot of information. But after reading that letter we gave you, the two seem to fit together, don't they?"

We all nodded.

"Did he ask anything else?" I wanted to know.

"Well, we told him about the letter we had found," Chloe said, "and its basic contents. He asked more about it, so we told him that you were planning to ask Marion to help you with it."

"It was about that time," said Rudy, wiping his mouth with a napkin, "that I started to wonder if this guy was for real. It seemed strange to me that he had come by himself. And his beard wasn't too well taken care of and his hair was kind of messed up. In fact, he sort of looked like he'd been sleeping in his clothes for the past week. Now normally I wouldn't hold that kind of thing against a man, but it just seemed a little unusual for an FBI agent."

"So Rudy asked him for his identification," Chloe said. "Then he got real nervous. He said he had to be on his way."

"He did pull out his wallet," said Rudy, "and showed us some sort of badge—but we never really got a good look at it."

"So knowing that he might go and talk to Marion," Chloe continued, "we gave him a call over at the library." Turning to Rudy, she asked, "Did the agent ever come to talk to Marion?"

"He sure did," nodded Rudy, "but since we'd warned him, he asked for identification right up front and wouldn't tell him anything as far as I know. Marion told the feller that if he wanted more information then he would need to come back with a partner."

"So he had a beard and messed up hair?" Brandon said. "He doesn't sound like either of the FBI agents that we met at home. I wonder who he was."

"You met some other agents?" asked Chloe. "When?"

"A couple of weeks ago," answered Shauna. "They said that the man who called Meg—the one who gave her that message—was missing. And so was the document that the message was written on. But neither of them had beards."

"Well, this guy," said Rudy, "was about my height and really skinny."

"Do you think he's the same guy who's been following us?" I asked.

"He could be," said Shauna. "He has a beard. And it's possible that his long hair was that wig."

"Maybe that's why his hair was messed up," Meg breathed.

"Now what is this?" asked Chloe. "A man has been following you?"

"That's right," I said. "We think he followed us just about everywhere we went."

"We first started catching glimpses of him in Kirtland," Brandon said, "last week when we were here. We just kept noticing this man with long, brown hair and a beard and a big yellowish straw hat."

"Then we saw him going into the lobby of our hotel in Rochester, New York!" said Shauna. "Just the day after we got there."

"And we found a car in the parking lot," said Brandon with more and more excitement. "And it had Ohio license plates and on the front seat was a copy of the document that included the message that Meg has."

"And then we saw the same car behind our hotel in Niagara Falls," I explained.

"We're not sure," said Shauna, "but we think that the same guy grabbed our room key from Brandon's shirt pocket and then stole the letter you gave us from our room. Nothing else was missing except for the letter."

Chloe seemed stunned. "Th-the letter *we* gave you?" she asked. "Just last week? It's been stolen?"

We all nodded.

"I don't suppose you had time to make a copy of it first," Rudy said.

We all shook our heads.

Then Shauna said, "Do you think you would recognize the voice of that fake FBI agent if you heard it?"

"It's possible," Rudy nodded. "Why? What do you have in mind?"

"Well," said Shauna, reaching for her computer bag, "we managed to record the voice of the man at our hotel in Niagara Falls. I have it on this computer."

She pulled out the computer and booted it up.

"How did you manage that?" Rudy wanted to know.

While we waited for the computer program to load, I told them how we forced the man to go to the front desk so that we could record his voice.

"Ingenious," Chloe said, shaking her head. "You kids are amazing!"

Shauna made a few clicks on the computer and then asked, "Are you ready?"

The recording was much clearer than I expected. There were a few seconds of just background noise before we heard anything. Then we heard footsteps getting closer.

"May I help you?" came a woman's voice. I recognized her as the lady who called herself Annie.

"Yes," said the man. "I need someone to move your hotel van at the back door. I inadvertently parked too close behind it and now someone else has parked too close behind me. I can't get out until one of you moves."

His voice sounded oddly familiar.

"Right away, sir," said Annie.

We heard her pick up the phone, push a couple of buttons, and then say, "Tyson, I need you move the van in the back. There's a gentleman here who can't get his car out."

She hung up the phone and said, "I do apologize for the inconvenience. It will be taken care of in just a moment."

We heard several footsteps moving away, then stopping and returning. I noticed that Rudy was beginning to nod his head up and down and that Brandon's mouth was wide open and so were his eyes.

"May I use your phone?" the man on the recording asked. "It's long distance, but I have a calling card number."

"Of course, sir," said Annie. We heard the phone being placed on the counter. The phone was picked up and we heard at least twenty buttons being pushed.

Then the man said, "Hello, this is FBI Agent Smith." There was a pause. "Have you been able to get the information yet?" Another pause. "No, I'm still working on getting the details of what the information is for, but I believe I'm close." A longer pause. Then he said, "I'd appreciate it if you could get that today, if at all possible. The family is due back tomorrow, so we haven't much time." A short pause and then, "Thank you, Mr. Shirley. Good-bye."

We heard the phone being hung up and then the footsteps going away until they disappeared completely. Then the recording ended.

Rudy was the first to speak. He said, "I do believe that was the man."

"I think you're right," said Chloe.

I looked at Brandon again. All the color had left his face.

"What?" I asked. He gulped hard, but didn't answer.

I looked at Shauna. She looked absolutely horrified. And Meg looked even worse.

"That was *Dr. Anthony*," Brandon breathed. His words hit me like a fist in the stomach.

CHAPTER 14

The Light Dawns

As soon as Brandon said the name "Dr. Anthony" I knew that he was right! How could I have not recognized his voice right from the start? Brandon did—and it looked to me like Shauna and Meg had also. Had my mind just been trying to block it all out?

Perhaps now is a good time to explain who Dr. Anthony is. First of all, I'm not sure he's really a doctor of *anything*. That's what he calls himself, but he's been lying to me and my family and everyone else about anything and everything for as long as we've known him. He claims to be a historian. We first met him three years ago when my family was visiting our Great-aunt Ella on her dairy farm in Iowa. We actually stayed there for a couple of months—which is a nightmare story of its own. Aunt Ella had a very old copy of the Book of Mormon, from the very first printing in 1830. Come to think about it, that means it was printed in that shop that we saw while we were in Palmyra, New York.

Anyway, Dr. Anthony had been bugging our Great-aunt Ella to let him borrow the book so he "could do some research" with it. She didn't want to let it out of the house. She told him that he could spend as much time as he wanted to with the book, but it had to stay in her farmhouse. He kept trying to get her to change her mind and then, eventually, he just stole the book. We got it back, but it turned out that what he was really after was a treasure map that he thought was with the book. He never found any treasure map and neither did we. What we *did* find, though, was this old sheet of paper. It looked like an important document that the Church would be interested in, so we donated it to them. We didn't really hear anything more about it until this Paul Mauer guy called us from the archive department a couple of weeks ago.

Well, Dr. Anthony had been inviting himself on our family vacations ever since. He showed up and ruined everything last year and now—as we just found out, it was beginning to look like he had been tagging along this year as well.

"Who is Dr. Anthony?" asked Rudy.

I'm sure that Chloe and Rudy were trying to figure out what was going on inside our four heads to make Shauna, Brandon, Meg, and me look horrified, shocked, scared, and bewildered—in *that* order.

"He's a historian 'slash' criminal," said Shauna, finally managing to make her tongue work. "He's been trying to steal old documents from us for the last three years."

"But he doesn't really want the documents," Brandon whispered. "He really just wants whatever treasure he thinks these documents will lead him to."

"Wait a minute!" I exclaimed. "How did he get out of *prison? Again?*"

"How does he *ever* get out?" Brandon asked.

Dr. Anthony was slimy. After he had been caught last year, I was convinced that I would never have to deal with him again. How wrong I was! The thought of him made me slightly nauseated. The remaining gourmet bologna sandwiches on the plate in the middle of the table suddenly didn't look that good anymore.

"I wonder how he got a copy of the document," Meg said.

"Oh, yeah," Brandon said. He got a distant look in his eyes, like he was trying to figure it out. Then he started slowly shaking his head back and forth. Finally he just heaved a sigh.

"Any guesses who this Mr. Shirley is?" Shauna asked.

165

"Do you think it's the same Shirley who works with Marion at the library?" Chloe suggested.

"I've never heard anyone call him *Mr.* Shirley before," said Rudy.

"Dr. Anthony is . . ." Brandon paused as he tried to come up with the right word. He had a look of disgust on his face.

Shauna finished the thought for him by saying, "He's dopey enough to make that mistake and never figure it out."

We all agreed.

About this time there came a knock at the door. It was Marion.

"Ah, hello!" Marion greeted us with a smile. "Nice to see you all again." Looking around he said, "But you're not all here, are you? Where are your parents?"

"They'll be here later," Shauna said, "with our youngest brother and sister."

"Did you tell that fake FBI agent anything?" Brandon asked.

Marion looked over at Brandon with surprise and said, "Well, you get right to the point, don't you? No, I didn't. Rudy here was kind enough to warn me, and so I insisted on seeing some ID or a warrant or something before I would answer any of his questions about you."

"What about Shirley?" I asked. "Would he have told this guy anything?"

Marion's smile faded a bit. "Shirley is another matter."

Rudy said with a laugh, "He *surely* is!"

We smiled in an attempt to be polite, but none of us were really in the mood for jokes.

"Why do you ask about Shirley?" Marion asked.

"Because we think Shirley might have been helping him," said Shauna. "Can we play a recording for you?"

"Of course," Marion said.

Shauna pulled out her computer again and played the recording for Marion.

"Does that sound like the man you talked to at the library?" Shauna asked Marion.

"Yes, ma'am," Marion said. "That certainly sounds like the same man to me."

"That's what we thought, too," said Rudy.

"And we think that 'Mr. Shirley' might actually be the same Shirley that works at the library," Brandon said.

"Because it looks like someone may have been trying to follow the clues laid out in that letter we found," said Rudy. "C'mon outside and take a look."

We all followed Rudy outside once more. It was early evening now. The sun was low enough in the sky that the shadow from the house fell across the spot where the broken tree limb was. Rudy explained his theory about how someone had been standing on the limb when it broke.

"Was this ladder here last night?" Marion asked.

"No," said Rudy. "I brought it out this morning when the police wanted a closer look up there where the limb broke off."

"Did they find anything?" Marion asked.

"Come over t'other side of the house," said Rudy. "I'll show you what they found."

"They found this hole?" Marion asked when we got there. "You didn't see it before?"

"I saw it all right," said Rudy. "In fact, I chased the fellers off who were digging it."

"So what did the police find, then?" asked Marion.

"They found that if you stand right here," said Rudy, "you can see right through the windows on both sides of the house." He now pointed right at the windows as he spoke. "And can you guess what is right in line with this here hole and those two windows?"

"The tree where the limb broke?" asked Marion with a smile.

"That's right," said Rudy. "So it looks like someone's been

diggin' here for buried treasure." Then Rudy asked, "Did you tell Shirley what you were working on for these folks?"

Marion smiled, "Yes, I did."

My heart sank.

"I knew it!" said Brandon. "Shirley has been helping Dr. Anthony."

"Who's Dr. Anthony?" asked Marion.

"They think that's the real name of the guy pretending to be an FBI agent," explained Rudy.

"Did Shirley know what you had figured out?" Shauna asked.

"Yes," Marion smiled again. "And I told him *exactly* what you asked me to find out for you." He was now smiling bigger than ever.

I couldn't figure out what he was so happy about! Was he in on it, too?

"You gotta joke brewing somewhere, Marion?" Rudy asked with a curious look. "What's going on inside that genius head of yours?"

"After the supposed FBI agent came into the library—" said Marion, "what did you call him? Dr. Anthony?—After he came into the library and I wouldn't tell him anything, I saw him out in the parking lot talking with Shirley. Now Shirley used to fancy himself something of a private detective. I don't know if you knew that, but he's always looking to solve whatever little mystery comes up."

"That's right," breathed Brandon. "I remember him saying something like that the day we first met him."

Marion nodded. "So when I saw the two of them together, I figured they were up to no good."

"So, do you think Shirley is trying to help Anthony steal the treasure?" Brandon asked.

"I don't think so," said Marion, "but he's surely convinced himself that this Anthony fellow is for real and he's just helping out."

"So what's the joke?" Rudy asked.

Turning to us, Marion said, "Do you remember what you asked me to find out for you?"

"Of course," I said, "we want to know where the sun comes up on whatever day it comes up the latest—January something."

"No," said Marion, shaking his head and smiling. "That's what *I* told you that you *really* wanted after I read the letter. *You* told *me* that you wanted it for December twenty-first, the shortest day of the year." Marion paused as his smile grew larger.

"Oh!" said Shauna suddenly, also with a big smile. "So you told Shirley where the sun comes up on December twenty-first?"

Marion nodded. I think the rest of us all suddenly realized what he was saying.

"That means they were digging in the wrong spot!" Brandon exclaimed.

"They probably shouldn't have been digging at all," smiled Marion. "The location of the sun is going to be different enough that I'm sure it will shine on some place in the attic."

"We probably just got very lucky that the windows lined up the way they did," Rudy said. His thumbs were in the sides of his belt and he looked very pleased with life. "That kept those fellers from digging up m'attic."

Marion agreed. "Let's go see what we can figure out," he suggested.

The first thing Marion wanted to do was go up in the attic. I had forgotten how much stuff was up there. Not only was it amazing that the two windows lined up with the tree outside, but it was also amazing that there just happened to be a clear shot from window to window so that they could see from one side of the attic to the other.

"I made sure there was an aisle between all the windows," explained Chloe, "so we could get as much natural light in here as possible."

169

From the attic window nearest the tree with the broken limb, Marion looked outside.

"It's a good thing the hill drops off so quickly on this side of the house," Marion said, "otherwise the trees would be too thick to let us see the horizon and determine where the sun will rise."

Marion pulled a folded piece of paper from his shirt pocket and opened it up. He had a drawing of the rolling hills on the horizon that almost perfectly matched what I could see through the scattered trees.

"This time of day is exactly what we needed," said Marion. "The setting sun behind us lights up the tops of those hills perfectly. And since the trees are now in the shadow of the house, we can see right through them."

Marion's drawing of the horizon had two large dots on it. Next to one he had written "12/21" and by the other was "1/10."

"What are those numbers for?" I asked.

"December twenty-first and January tenth," Marion explained. He smiled to himself and said, "Now the paper that Shirley got ahold of only had this marking here." Marion pointed to the dot next to "12/21."

Marion laughed softly and said, "And he used it well. That tree over there with the broken branch is perfectly lined up with this point on the horizon." Marion held his arm out straight toward the tree and then turned his body and looked out the opposite window. "Amazing," he smiled.

"Does everything line up with that hole in the yard?" asked Rudy.

"Straight as an arrow," said Marion. Turning back to the window where he stood, he said, "But let's find out where the real location is, shall we?"

Marion held his drawing up to the window and carefully looked back and forth several times between the page and the row of trees outside. The thing that amazed me the most about the drawing was the fact the mark for December 21 was almost at the bottom of a steep valley between a couple of the hills, but the mark for January 10 was quite a distance up the hillside.

"Wow," I said. "It's amazing how much of a difference three weeks make."

"It surely is," Marion smiled. I couldn't tell if he was making a joke or not. "It makes a big enough difference to put a hole in the yard on the other side of the house, instead of hole in the floor or the wall in here."

"Do you think it will be so different that it could be clear down on the floor?" I asked. The thought surprised me.

"Just giving it a rough estimate," said Marion, "I'd say the mark is either going to be very low on the wall or else on the floor right next to it." He spoke slowly and looked back and forth several times between the tree outside and the opposite wall. "I'm going to head outside for a few minutes," Marion said as he started down the stairs. We all followed.

"I'll be in the parlor if anyone needs me," Chloe said as the rest of us went outside.

We helped Marion adjust the ladder a few feet from its original position. Brandon and I each held one leg of the ladder while Marion climbed up and carefully tied a bright red ribbon on a certain branch of the tree. He then looked back and forth several times between the tree and the window.

"Any chance we could open up those windows in the attic?" Marion asked Rudy.

"Not a problem," said Rudy.

"I can't tell if I'm in the correct spot or not," Marion said. Looking down at me he asked, "You're Jeff, aren't you?"

"Yes."

"Will you take this paper up into the attic and help me get this ribbon lined up with the point on the horizon marked January tenth?" Marion dropped the paper to me.

"Sure!" I said.

"I'll go open the window," Rudy offered, heading into the house.

"Now we need to hurry a bit," Marion said. "We want to get this location marked before the sun leaves the top of those hills."

I followed Rudy into the house and up the stairs. Rudy went to the window and removed the latches. Then he grabbed onto a small hand crank at one side of the windowsill and turned it several times. The window swung outward from a hinge along the side until it was sticking straight out from the side of the house.

Using the paper as my guide, I called through the open window over to where Marion stood on the ladder. The ribbon he had tied onto the tree was actually already pretty close to where it was supposed to be, but after two or three attempts, he had it in a place that perfectly matched the drawing he had made. It turned out that the drawing was extremely accurate. Luckily, the outline of the hills in the distance was really quite distinct and easy to match up with the drawing that Marion had made.

I watched as Marion climbed down from the ladder. Calling back up to where I stood, Marion said, "Now we wait until dark. You can close the window—we're done with it."

"Okay," I called down to him.

But before he closed the window, Rudy called down to Marion and asked, "You don't think we can make a good enough guess to make a small opening in the wall?"

"It's touch and go whether we're talking about the wall or the floor, Rudy," Marion said. "Now I reckon you don't want to be tearing into one and then find out we should have been inside the other."

"You've got that right," Rudy agreed. "I already have a hole in my yard that I didn't really want!"

Rudy cranked the knob several times and the window swung shut once more. He latched it and we both went back downstairs.

Back inside the kitchen Marion said, "I brought a flashlight with me that has a concentrated beam. I reckon that will do the job as soon as it's a little darker."

"Once we mark the spot," Rudy said, "are you feelin' up to helping us make a hole and do a little treasure huntin'?"

Marion smiled and said, "My, my, Rudy, it does appear to me as if you've gotten yourself worked up about this adventure just a tad."

Rudy smiled and nodded. Finally he said, "I suppose you're right about that, Marion. I admit I didn't put too much stock in the whole thing last week when it first came up, but the idea has grown on me just a bit since then."

"And if there is some treasure still hidden up there," Marion asked, "what will you do with it?"

"Treasure?" said Rudy. "Oh, whatever it's worth and whoever it belongs to doesn't concern me s'much as just having a little bit of intrigue associated with this old place." He looked around the room affectionately as he spoke.

There was no doubt in my mind that he was telling the absolute truth. I found myself wondering what Mom would do with it, if we found some treasure and everyone decided it belonged to her.

As we sat around the kitchen table talking, Chloe came in and served us all some fresh peach pie. It was at least as good as I remembered it from the week before—maybe even better. As we were finishing up, Marion said, "I reckon it's dark enough outside now that we ought to give this a try."

I felt a chill run up my spine as I thought about what we were about to do. Brandon and I held the ladder for Marion again as he climbed up with the flashlight. Rudy and the girls were up in the attic so they could mark where the flashlight beam pointed.

Chloe went into the parlor to wait. "You just tell me what you find," she said, wearily.

Rudy opened the window again so that he and Marion could talk to each other.

"I've got it," Marion called over to the window. "I'm holding it as steady as I can!"

About a half minute later Meg came to the window and said, "Rudy says it's okay now. You can come down." She was shading her eyes with her hand.

Marion switched off the flashlight and asked, "Did he mark it?"

"Uh-huh," said Meg, blinking several times. I don't think her eyes had adjusted to the dark outside the window yet.

"Is it on the wall or on the floor?" Marion asked.

"On the wall," Meg said. "Right next to the floor."

"We'll be right there," Marion said and he started to climb down the ladder. On his way down he said to Brandon and me, "I figured it was going to be close."

As we walked into the house together, Marion said, "I'm glad it's on the wall. From the looks of that floor, I'd reckon it would have been a lot more work to try to make an opening in that solid wood up there."

If the floor would have been more work, then I'm really glad, too. Making a hole in the wall was bad enough. It turned out that the wall was covered with thick plaster, but inside the plaster was a heavy wire mesh that broke three of Rudy's saw blades before he was finally able to cut a square opening that was about ten inches on each side.

"Take a look at these solid wood planks in here," Rudy said to Marion.

Marion shook his head in amazement and said, "They look original to me."

"Do you think so?" I asked. To me that made it sound like we might have a chance that Elias Franzen's treasure was still there.

"Of course," Rudy explained. "See how they're not cut square and they still have the bark on the sides?"

"They just took a big log and cut it into planks," Marion said. "Back then they wouldn't have bothered to take the time to make the boards uniform like they do now." Turning back to Rudy, Marion asked, "So how thick is that plank?"

"It's almost two inches," Rudy said. "And there's a big enough gap between these two that you can see the original side-to-side planking they put up on the outside."

"That's not what you see from the outside now, is it?" asked Marion.

"Naw," said Rudy. "Somebody put up some wood siding right over the top of it years ago."

I was starting to get a little impatient with their conversation. I looked over at Brandon and saw that he was going absolutely nuts! As soon as Rudy and Marion both took a breath at the same time, Brandon blurted out, "Can you see the *treasure?*"

"I don't see anything," Rudy said, "but let me see if I can get my hand in there."

He slowly and carefully put his fingers in between the two planks that were running up and down.

"There's a big gap between this plank and the siding," Rudy said as he wriggled his fingers farther behind the plank. Then he stopped short and said, "I think I can feel something smooth back there— like leather."

He pulled his hand out, looked at Meg and said, "My hands are just too big, little lady. Do you think you could put your hand in there and pull out whatever is back there?"

"I can try," said Meg. "My mom says that I have small hands."

"Well, that's a good thing right now," Marion said.

Meg cautiously put her hand inside the wall where Rudy said that he had felt something.

"I can feel it," she said. She grunted a couple of times and then said, "It's kind of stuck."

"Keep trying," Rudy encouraged her.

Brandon looked like he was going to explode. I almost laughed when I looked at him, but I didn't dare.

Finally Meg said, "I got it!"

We all exhaled at the same time. I don't think anyone realized how tense we were until we all heard the sound. Then we laughed.

"Here it is," Meg said. In her hand she held a brown leather pouch that looked sort of like Mom's wallet, only about half as thick. She handed it to Rudy.

"It has the initials 'E. F.' on it," Rudy said, wiping the dust off.

We all jumped at the same time when we heard Chloe's voice from behind us. We hadn't heard her come up the stairs and the last we knew she was in the parlor by herself.

"There is someone here to see you, Rudy," Chloe said with a shaky voice.

We all turned to see Chloe standing at the top of the stairs with a man right behind her. He had a scraggly beard and was dressed in a suit that looked like he had slept in it for the past several nights.

"Agent Smith?" Rudy said.

"That's Dr. Anthony," Brandon corrected him with disgust in his voice.

"He has a gun," Chloe said quietly.

Anthony held up the gun so that we could all see it. Up till then, it was hidden behind Chloe.

"I'll be happy to take that off your hands," Anthony said to Rudy with a sneer.

"Now don't be doing something you'll regret as soon as it's done," Rudy said.

"The only thing I might regret is shooting someone with this gun," snarled Anthony, waving it around. "So give me what's in your hand before I do."

Standing up slowly and walking across the attic, Rudy handed the pouch to Anthony without a word. Anthony smiled that sick smile that I knew all too well and quickly disappeared down the stairs.

CHAPTER 15

The Chase

We all stood in stunned silence for several seconds.

"Are we just going to let him get away with that?" Marion asked finally.

"We?" asked Chloe.

"Not me!" yelled Brandon suddenly, bolting for the stairs.

"Brandon! What are you doing?" Shauna called after him. His only answer was the sound of his feet jumping down the stairs two at a time.

"Looks like I'm baby-sitting again," I called over my shoulder to everyone else as I headed after Brandon.

"Rudy, you call the police," I heard Marion say from behind me. Following me down the stairs he added, "I didn't do all this treasure huntin' just to watch the reward vanish into the night."

Brandon was heading for the front door with me and Marion hot on his heels. Pushing through the screen door, Brandon yelled, "There he goes!"

Marion and I got outside just in time to see a car pass underneath a streetlight and disappear over the hill.

"It's the putrid green car!" I yelled. "It *was* Anthony all along!"

"Let's go get him!" Marion said, scurrying around the side of the house. "My car is over here."

Brandon jumped into the front seat and I got in the back. Marion backed up the car quickly and turned in front of the house, jerking to a stop as he shifted the car into drive. As the car was stopping, the door into the backseat flew open.

Shauna yelled, "We're sticking together on this one!" as she and Meg climbed into the backseat with me. "I *am* my brothers' keeper—both of you—and I'm not about to let you out of my sight."

Marion accelerated down the graveled driveway toward the street as soon as the door slammed shut.

"And you're your sister's keeper, too," Meg said.

"Yes, I am," Shauna said, leaning over to hug Meg. Then, being "the keeper" that she was, Shauna said, "Put your seat belts on, guys!"

Marion's car sped up the hill in the same direction as Anthony's green stink bomb.

"Do you see him?" I asked, stretching my neck in an effort to see past Marion's head.

"Not sure yet," said Marion. He sounded intense. "There are a couple of cars up ahead, though."

"I think that's him," Brandon said, leaning forward and looking straight ahead.

"I'm sure he's headed for the main road," said Marion. "That gives us three blocks to catch up to him and see which way he turns."

"What if we don't get there in time?" I asked.

"Then we head for the Interstate," said Marion. "Only a fool would stay here in town."

Brandon and I looked at each other and both said, "He'll stay in town!"

"What's an Interstate?" asked Meg.

"That's what we call the freeway," Shauna explained.

We were only about half a block from the main highway when Brandon called, "There he is!"

Sure enough, the lights along the highway made the green color stand out boldly as the car turned right at the corner ahead of us.

"Is he heading toward the Interstate?" Shauna asked.

"Yes, he is," Marion nodded.

I didn't realize how fast we had been going until Marion had to stop at the intersection with the highway. I had to put my hands up against the back of Marion's seat to keep my head from bouncing against it.

"Sorry 'bout that," Marion said as the car finally stopped. A single car whizzed by in front of us before Marion was able to pull out on the highway just behind it.

"Looks like he's just two cars ahead of us," Brandon said.

We were on the main road through Kirtland and everybody around there called it "the highway," but it really wasn't much of a road. It only had a single lane of cars going in each direction.

"Do you think you can pass this guy?" Brandon asked about the unknown car in front of us.

"I doubt it," said Marion. "Not with this traffic."

So even though only one car was between us and Anthony, it looked like it was going to stay that way for a while; there were far too many cars coming from the other direction to be able to pass. Actually, though, the thought of being right behind Anthony didn't excite me too much. I kind of liked the idea of being shielded just a bit.

"I hope he doesn't get away from us," Brandon said. "That car better stay close to him."

No one responded. We probably all agreed with Brandon, but there really wasn't anything we could do about it either way. As if on cue, however, the car in front of us almost instantly started slowing down, creating a bigger and bigger gap between him and the green car. We had passed the Kirtland Temple at this point and were heading down a steep hill. Anthony's car was already to the bottom of the hill, and we could see it starting to climb back up the other side of the gulch. I noticed that there were no cars in front of him to slow him down.

"What's this guy *doing?*" Brandon asked in disgust. And then, as if the driver in front of us might be able to hear him, he yelled, "C'mon! Move it! We gotta catch that putrid guy!"

"Do you know what *putrid* means?" Shauna asked Meg.

"Yes," said Meg, matter-of-factly. "Stinky!"

Marion glanced over at Brandon and said, "I thought it was the green car that was putrid."

"The guy inside is putrid, too," Brandon said.

Marion nodded silently for a moment before saying, "I reckon you're right."

As I noticed how close we were to the car in front of us, I thought about the definition of *tailgating* that I had learned in my driver's ed class a few months earlier. In my mind I could hear my teacher's voice saying, "To tailgate is to drive dangerously close behind another vehicle." To be honest, I was starting to feel the danger he was talking about. I was getting really nervous.

After a few seconds, Marion began to slow, creating a large gap.

"What's wrong?" Brandon asked in surprise. Apparently he wasn't bothered by tailgating. He looked over at Marion with wide eyes.

"I reckon maybe that driver didn't like me being so close to his rear bumper," said Marion. "I'm hoping that if I back off a little, then maybe he'll speed back up."

We were climbing the hill now, and Anthony was out of sight. The road curved to the right as we continued to climb. I could tell Brandon was starting to get really uptight.

"What if we lose him?" Brandon wailed.

No one had a response for that.

After finally going around the curve and getting to the top of the hill, the road widened to two lanes, and we were able to move around the car in front of us that had been going so slow. We couldn't go far, though, because there was a red light at the first intersection.

"Do you see him?" I asked, leaning forward and toward the middle of the car to get a better look.

"That might be him in front of us," Marion said.

As we pulled up behind the car stopped at the red light, Brandon said with excitement, "I think it is!"

"It's putrid green, all right," I said.

"But the license plates are different again," Brandon said.

"It didn't have Pennsylvania tags before?" asked Marion.

"Pennsylvania?" I asked. "Does he steal license plates everywhere he goes?"

"At first they were Ohio," Brandon explained, "and then New York."

"What about the sticker with the peace sign in the back window?" I asked. "Is it still there?"

It was too dark to tell. When the light changed to green, Marion was careful to stay close enough to Anthony's car so that no other car could get in between us again.

"Is he still heading toward the Interstate?" Shauna asked.

"Yes," Marion nodded. "It's about three blocks ahead."

We continued to follow Anthony's car through the traffic for the next two blocks, stopping at red lights at each intersection. Then, about a half block before the freeway entrance, the car turned into the parking lot of a hotel. Marion slowed down dramatically and then turned slowly into the same parking lot.

"I don't want to get close enough for him to see us," said Marion, "so I'm going to drive around the back of the building."

"We can't let him out of our sight!" said Brandon, sounding desperate. "He gets away too easily! He's done it to us before."

"Let Brandon and me get out here and watch where he goes," I suggested.

Marion slowed the car, but didn't say anything. I think he was trying to decide if he thought it was a good idea or not. But Brandon didn't wait for a response. As soon as the car stopped, he jumped out and hid in some bushes.

"Hey!" called Marion. "What are you doing?" he asked as the car door slammed shut.

"I'll go with him," I said, quickly jumping out and scampering over to where Brandon was hidden.

Marion's car didn't move for a moment, but then started around the back of the building.

"Where is he?" I asked Brandon, turning my attention back toward the parking lot.

"He parked near the far end of the row," Brandon said, "but he hasn't gotten out yet."

"Is that him?" I asked. I saw the outline of a man stand up and head for the side entrance of the hotel. He was moving farther away from us.

"That's him," Brandon breathed. He sounded determined.

"Good," I said, thinking we could relax. "We can call the police and let them find him inside."

Brandon didn't say anything.

"Do you think the hotel manager will let us use the phone to call the police?" I asked.

Brandon still didn't say anything. Then I realized why. Staying behind a long row of bushes, Brandon had made his way down the length of the parking lot. I hadn't realized that he was gone until he darted out from behind the bushes and headed across the parking lot toward the car. Knowing that Shauna would be unhappy if we didn't stay together, I ran as hard as I could to catch up to him.

"There's the peace sign," Brandon said, pointing at the corner of the rear window of the green car. "It's him all right."

Even in the well-lit parking lot, the sticker was a little hard to see because it was on the inside of the window. I leaned over for a closer look. When I had seen it for myself and now knew for sure that it had been Anthony all along, I looked back to say something to Brandon—but he was gone again!

This time I saw him disappearing around the corner of the hotel where Anthony had gone. When I got to the corner, I saw Brandon standing, holding the door to the hotel open, impatiently motioning for me to hurry over to where he was. But as soon as he knew that I had seen him, he vanished inside. I ran like crazy again, afraid that I might lose him. When I got to the door and pulled it open, I found Brandon just inside the building holding another door open at the bottom of a set of concrete stairs. He had his index finger against his lips. I could hear the sound of footsteps climbing the stairs above us.

When we heard the sound of a door opening and clicking shut, Brandon hissed, "Let's go!" and headed up the stairs two at a time.

"How do we know what floor he's on?" I asked as loud as I dared.

"I counted sixteen footsteps after I saw that he was turning the corner at the second floor," Brandon whispered loudly. "So we just count from there."

It turned out not to be too hard. There were exactly 16 steps between the second and third floors—and that was as high as they went. Brandon opened the door as quietly as he could, peering around the corner. Before I had any idea what he was doing, he took off on a run again—but he was amazingly quiet. As I came out of the stairway and began following him, I saw that he was stooped way over and hugging one wall as he ran. As soon as I saw what was down the hall, I did the exact same thing.

Anthony was about halfway down the hall, standing at a door, fumbling with various other things he was pulling out of his pockets, obviously trying to find his room key. Along the same side of the hall where he was standing was a roll-away bed. Stooping down and staying close to the wall kept us well hidden from Anthony's view. Brandon stopped short as soon as he was next to the roll-away, and I snuck in right behind him. Within a couple of seconds we heard the door unlock and then the door slam shut again.

"Good job, Brandon!" I whispered. "Let's get the room number and go back and find everybody else. We can wait outside and watch his car until the police come." I looked at the door and said, "It's room 313. Let's go!"

"I'm not waiting outside," Brandon said, standing up and moving quickly toward Anthony's door.

"*What?*" I hissed. "You're crazy."

"Look," Brandon said, still moving toward the door. "I want to get inside there before he opens up that pouch. Whatever is in there could be long gone by the time the police get here."

I couldn't believe what I was hearing. Nor could I imagine what Brandon thought he was going to do. I literally jumped when he knocked loudly on the door. I'm sure my eyes just about bugged completely out of my head as he did it. As soon as he had knocked, though, Brandon immediately ran past me and hid behind the roll-away bed again. I was so stunned by what he was doing, I almost didn't follow him. I quickly came to myself, though, and scrambled over behind him.

"*What* are you *doing?*" I hissed in complete fear and amazement.

His response was to stretch his mouth out into a straight line across his face and then hold up a small card in front of me, as though that should make everything perfectly clear. It was a card that listed the business hours for the family history center where we had first learned that Elias Franzen's home in Kirtland was still standing.

I had no idea what that card was supposed to mean. Was he planning to go up against a man with a gun, when we were armed with nothing more than a single business card? Was I supposed to figure out if the family history center was still open and run there for help? Obviously, neither of those options made any sense, but that's *all* I could think of! I'm sure the expression on my face reflected my complete bewilderment. I turned the palms of my hands upward as a further sign of my confusion.

Before I could ask Brandon if he would *please* be kind enough to give me some other clue besides the business card, I heard Anthony's door open and the two of us froze in silence behind the bed. Brandon watched Anthony's every movement through the narrow space between the roll-away and the wall. At the same moment that I heard Anthony give a disgusted, "Hhhrmff," Brandon stood and charged toward the door. His sudden movement made me jump again and I almost fell over.

Brandon was moving without a sound once more. He reached the door just as it was about to slam shut. I thought he was going to try to stop the door from closing, but instead, to my amazement, carefully holding one edge of the business card, he inserted it in the gap between the door and the doorjamb, just as the door slammed against it, keeping the door from latching shut! Then, in order to keep the door from bouncing, he grabbed the doorknob with his other hand and held it tightly in place. I think my chin literally hit my chest as I watched.

"*Where* did you learn *that?*" I hissed after walking over to where he stood, still holding the card and the doorknob.

"You don't want to know," Brandon whispered.

Of course I wanted to know. What was he thinking? But Brandon was ignoring me now and listening intently as he slowly opened the door enough to create about a two-inch gap. We heard another door click shut. We looked at each other with excitement, thinking about what this might mean.

"Did he just go into the bathroom and close the door?" I asked.

Brandon nodded without answering and immediately began pushing the door open wider. We both pushed our way inside. There was a small sink area right behind the door. It was like a short entryway. It was dark, but we could see light coming out from under a doorway that was obviously the bathroom. There was a single lamp on in the main part of the room, but it didn't shine into the hallway very well.

"Help me look," Brandon whispered as he made his way into the room.

The spring hinges on the door made it try to close by itself, so I had to stay at the door. I was planning on holding it *wide* open so that we could get out of there as fast as possible. I watched for a couple of seconds as Brandon started sifting quickly through stacks of papers and clothes on the dresser—that was all I could see.

"Help me!" Brandon hissed again, so I let the door close until the latch touched the doorjamb, but didn't latch.

I was amazed at what I found in the rest of the room. Besides the dresser, there was a large bed, a table, and two chairs—and they were all a complete mess. Papers and clothes were scattered everywhere and on top of everything.

"Check on the table," Brandon ordered me.

I looked over the top layer of junk and decided that was as close as I wanted to get to Anthony's garbage.

"Maybe he left it on the counter by the sink," I said, walking quickly back to the dark entryway. I didn't want to knock anything over by mistake, so I waited a moment until my eyes adjusted to the dark. I was practically petrified thinking about the fact that Anthony was just on the other side of the dark door. I tried not to think about it.

Then I saw it! I put my hand carefully over the pouch to make sure it felt like what I expected it be: soft, old leather. I was sure I had found what we were after. Grabbing the pouch and moving as quickly as I dared back to where Brandon was, I held it up for him to see. He glanced up and immediately clenched his fist with excitement.

Just as we started for the door, the bathroom door opened and a dark figure moved toward us. I froze in my tracks, realizing that we now had absolutely no chance of getting past Anthony and to the door.

"What?" Anthony bellowed in disbelief. Then he snarled, "How did you get in here?"

As his eyes darted fanatically back and forth between me and Brandon, I took the opportunity to take several steps backward and hide the pouch behind me.

"We have a flying hippo!" Brandon said defiantly.

Now Anthony's eyes locked solidly on Brandon. He stared at him with total disgust and finally said, "You always do react stupidly when you're trapped."

Then he looked back at me and said, "And don't think I don't know what you're hiding behind you. It's mine. Now give it back."

I felt my eyes get really wide as I continued to move backwards. Anthony looked determined as he started to move toward us.

"You two are guilty of breaking and entering," Anthony said. "I should call the police right now. At least that will keep you from being guilty of yet another crime: *theft!*"

"So . . . is breaking and entering like what *you* did at Chloe and Rudy's house?" Brandon asked. Anthony's eyes narrowed and one side of his upper lip began to curl. "And let's see," Brandon went on, "the fact that you actually *stole* something means that—unlike us—you *are* guilty of theft. We're just here to give you one less thing to end up in jail for!"

Anthony stopped moving toward us and looked around the room. Then Anthony scowled.

"But you were at Chloe and Rudy's last night, too, weren't you?" Brandon said.

Anthony didn't answer.

"What is someone guilty of when they dig a huge hole on someone else's property?" Brandon asked.

Anthony's eyes narrowed again.

"How dopey is that?" Brandon said. I couldn't figure out why

Brandon was trying to provoke this guy. He was going to make things worse than they already were.

"Not nearly as dopey as you might think," Anthony defended himself, still with a scowl. "When the Mormons left Nauvoo, do you know where they put all their valuables that they couldn't take with them?" Not waiting for an answer, Anthony said, "Down the *privy*, that's where!" We just stared at him. "You know what a privy is, don't you? It's an outhouse."

I continued to stare.

"*Sick!*" Brandon said. I had to agree. Then Brandon said, "What does *that* have to do with *this?*"

"It's just *possible*," said Anthony with growing distaste for our existence, "that the spot marked in the yard is where an outhouse was 170 years ago! That's what!"

"I will say it again," said Brandon. "How dopey is that? Who would put a pouch full of money down the outhouse?"

"Is that what's in it?" Anthony asked, suddenly remembering what this was all about. "Have you opened it?" he asked me.

I didn't say anything, but just took another step backward. I was almost at the window now.

Then Anthony said, "Just give it back to me and I won't hurt you."

"You couldn't hurt us if you tried," Brandon said.

I wanted to grab Brandon and stick one of Anthony's dirty socks in his mouth. I couldn't believe what he was saying! Was he actually *trying* to make Anthony mad? It was my opinion that he certainly *would* be able to hurt us if he really wanted to! I wanted to remind Brandon that *this lunatic had a gun!* But I didn't want to remind Anthony about it because so far he hadn't bothered to pull it out again. So I was hoping maybe he had forgotten, too—at least for minute. I decided to try a different strategy.

"I have just one question," I said. My voice sounded funny to me.

"What's that?" asked Anthony.

"How did you get out?" I asked.

That made Anthony smile. He even seemed to relax for a moment. Then he said with almost a little bit of pride in his voice, "I am a citizen of the United States of America. My government protects me."

I just stared back at him. Brandon was still behind me, so I didn't know what he was up to.

"Those fools couldn't prove that I had done anything wrong," Anthony said, shaking his head from side to side, "so they let me go. They turned me back over to the United States." Then his face clouded over again, "Eventually."

Anthony looked off into space for a moment, and I got the impression he was remembering something that he would have preferred not to remember ever again.

"And because they had no proof," Anthony said, still sounding a little unhappy, "*our* government let me go free as well."

Then, turning his attention back to the current situation, Anthony said, "Now give me back that pouch." He started to move toward us again and so Brandon and I both backed up against the drapes covering the window.

Just when I thought Anthony was going to come straight at us, he surprised me by picking up one of the chairs at the table. I watched in confusion as he walked backwards with it. Then he wedged the chair under the knob and against the door. It clicked shut when the chair bumped into it.

Anthony's head popped up and he said to us, "Leaving the door open for a quick getaway, were you?" Then with that demented smile that I had seen far too many times, he added, "Too bad for you."

Keeping his eyes on us, he fumbled around at the door until he turned the dead bolt and moved the overnight safety latch into place. Then he came toward us again.

"I'm just making sure you two don't get any ideas," Anthony sneered.

Without warning Brandon yelled, "There's more than one way out of this room!" At the same time he said it, I heard the curtains being torn open. I turned to see what Brandon was doing. With the curtains drawn back, he quickly grabbed the window latch and pulled with all his might. His whole body jerked to a halt when the window was open only about four inches. Brandon pulled again, but with no more luck than the first time: the window wouldn't open any wider. In frustration, Brandon thrust the palm of his hand hard against the window screen, sending it tumbling to the ground below.

Anthony began to laugh. That was a sound that I hadn't heard for a year and had been sure that I would never hear again. It was nauseating. "Now what?" Anthony sneered. "Don't you see that the Andrews brothers are out of options? Again?"

Anthony started toward us one more time. "Just give it to me," he said calmly, "and you can both go home."

"No way," said Brandon.

"Fine," said Anthony without feeling. He suddenly turned and went back into the darkened sink area. When he turned back to us a second later I saw what I had been hoping to avoid—the gun. He was holding it casually in one hand. "I was hoping that you two would be reasonable," Anthony said, coming toward us, "but I guess I should have known better."

He stopped about ten feet away from us, his eyes darting wildly back and forth between me and Brandon. Then he focused on me and said, "There's no way you're getting out of here with that. The only thing you have to decide is how much I'm going to hurt you before you give it to me."

I looked at the gun in his hand. He wasn't pointing it at us yet, but I didn't want to push my luck. I figured he was right—we had

190

no chance. Slowly, I brought the pouch out from behind me and set it on the table.

Anthony smiled crookedly. "Now you're being sensible," he said.

Brandon started to lunge for the pouch and that's when Anthony got mad. He immediately pointed the gun right at Brandon and yelled, "Stop!"

Amazingly, Brandon did just that.

Anthony stared at him for a moment and then finally said, "I can't trust you to be smart, can I?"

Brandon responded with, "I can't trust you to be anything but a crook, can I?"

That made Anthony even madder. "Sit in that chair," he ordered, pointing the gun at the one still at the table.

Brandon hesitated.

"Do it!" Anthony shouted.

Brandon moved to the chair and sat down. Reaching over to the dresser, Anthony grabbed a roll of duct tape that I had not noticed before and threw it to me.

"Tie him up," Anthony commanded. "Tape his legs to each of the chair legs and tape his arms to the arms of the chair—and hurry!"

I moved as quickly as I could, fumbling first with the plastic wrap covering the new roll of tape. At first I only wrapped Brandon's arms and legs with a single layer, but Anthony made me add at least two more layers to each. As I was finishing up, Anthony retrieved the first chair from the doorway and brought it over next to the open window.

"You'll never get away with this," Brandon said.

Anthony looked tired. "Shut up!" he yelled. "For once!"

Then Anthony looked at me and ordered, "Put a piece across his mouth."

After I put the tape across Brandon's mouth, Anthony said to

191

me, "Sit down." After I sat in the chair, he said, "Now do your own legs and one of your arms."

I did as I was told.

"Now don't do anything stupid," Anthony said. Still holding the gun in one hand, he held the loose end of the tape in his teeth and started to pull a piece off of it so that he could tape up my other arm.

Just then I heard a sound that made my heart jump into my throat. From outside the window I heard a voice call, "Brandon! Jeff! I see you! Are you okay?" It was Meg.

I turned my head and leaned it against the glass, looking down into the parking lot. There Meg stood, two stories below, looking frantically up at us. Almost without thinking, I reached over to where the pouch lay on the table next to me. With my legs and one arm taped to the chair, I was barely able to reach it. In a single motion, I scooped up the pouch and tossed it out the open window. Moving my face as close to the opening as I could get it, I yelled, "Meg! Quick! Grab the pouch!" I watched with excitement as it turned end over end and landed in a bush about two feet from where she stood.

CHAPTER 16

The Root of Lehi's Tree

Anthony shrieked. He sounded like a *girl!* We had heard him scream like that before. Brandon and I would regularly laugh about it whenever we remembered his screaming. But it had been so long since we had heard him, that I had begun to think that he didn't really sound as much like a girl as I had remembered. I was wrong. He did. I almost started to laugh, but that came to a quick halt when Anthony suddenly charged straight at me. I tried to move out of his way, but all I could really do was just lean to one side. I held my free arm up to protect my face. But I soon realized that he wasn't coming after me—he was headed for the window.

Sticking his face into the opening, he screamed at Meg, "You stay right there! That's mine! I'm coming down right now!"

Then Anthony immediately turned and ran for the door and began fumbling with the locks. Brandon and I watched him. I wanted out of the room as soon as possible, but I didn't want to draw attention to myself until he was gone. Anthony finally yanked the door open and charged into the hallway.

As soon as the door slammed shut, I turned my face to the window opening again and yelled, "Meg! Run! He's coming!"

She went rigid for a moment. Then she reached into the bush and picked up the pouch.

"We're stuck in here!" I yelled. "We'll be down as fast as we can!"

Meg started looking around frantically as if trying to decide where to go, then she bolted across the parking lot. I smiled as I saw her pink backpack bouncing around on her shoulders as she ran.

"Mmmpff!" Brandon said through the tape on his mouth. His eyes were wide open and he was glaring at me. With my free hand I peeled the tape off his face, then ripped the tape from one of Brandon's arms as quickly as I could. When his arm was free, we both began working to free ourselves.

"Jeff," Brandon grunted in frustration, "did you have to put so much tape on?"

I ignored him. I was too busy working on my ankles now. Brandon and I both freed ourselves at almost exactly the same time. I looked out the window and saw a police car with flashing red and blue lights in the parking lot.

"We're coming down right now!" I yelled through the four-inch opening.

Brandon headed for the door and I was right on his heels. I figured it had probably taken us at least a full minute to free ourselves from the duct tape. I worried about what might have happened in that amount of time.

The hallway and stairs were deserted. We ran as fast as we could, taking the stairs two at a time and crashing through the side door of the hotel into the parking lot. As we ran toward the front corner of the hotel, I heard Shauna yell, "Jeff! Brandon!"

We stopped and turned as she came running up to us.

"I just saw Anthony running into the woods," she said, pointing.

We were surprised by that. "Really?" I said.

"Yeah," Shauna explained. "I was coming around the back of the hotel when he came out the same door you guys just came out of. He was running up to the front, but then I think the police car scared him."

We looked in the direction of the front of the hotel. Even

though we couldn't see the police car, we could see the flashing red and blue emergency lights reflecting off the cars in the parking lot. We all started walking quickly in that direction.

"At first he waited at the corner of the building," Shauna explained. "He peeked around the corner several times and then he ran off into the woods." She pointed toward the far end of the parking lot as she spoke.

"We better tell the police," I said, as we rounded the corner.

"Do you think Dr. Anthony has the pouch with him?" Shauna asked.

"No," I said. "I threw it out the window to Meg."

"What?" said Shauna, a bit confused. "I left her in the lobby with Marion. What was she doing outside?"

As we approached the police car, I looked around for Meg, but she was nowhere to be seen. It was then that I first realized that she had run off in the same direction that Anthony had gone.

"Meg!" I called as I neared the place where she had been standing under the window. I turned toward the end of the parking lot where she had been running and cupped my hands around my mouth. "Meg!" I called again as loud as I could.

Brandon was spinning in small circles just a few feet away. He was looking desperately this way and that. "Meg, where are you!" he called.

I looked in the bushes where I had seen the pouch fall, but it was no longer there. I thought I had seen her pick it up, but I just wanted to make sure.

Marion came running out of the hotel lobby. "Where's your younger sister?" he asked with wide eyes. "She was in the lobby with me while I was on the phone with the police dispatcher, but when I hung up—she was gone! I turned around and she was gone."

"She's got to be close by here somewhere," I said to Brandon. "I saw her run off in that direction." I pointed toward the trees past the end of the parking lot as I spoke.

One of the police officers interrupted us by saying, "Whoa! Whoa! Whoa!" We all stopped and turned to him. "Now what's going on here?" he asked. "Who called the police?"

"That was me, officer," Marion said.

"Where's the thief?" asked the officer.

"He ran off into the woods over there," Shauna said, pointing.

"How long ago?" asked the officer.

"Just a minute or so," said Shauna.

"Grab the flashlights," said one officer to the other.

"But our little sister is missing!" Brandon said, sounding frantic.

The officer turned back around. "Your sister? How old is she?"

"She's eleven," I answered. "We got into the guy's hotel room and found what he had stolen from us. Then I threw it out the window to her and she took off running that way."

"Why did she run?" asked Marion.

"Because Jeff had taped himself and me to the chairs!" Brandon answered. The way Brandon said it made both Marion and the officers a little confused. "We couldn't get down here before Anthony was going to get here, so Jeff called out the window and told her to run."

"I saw her go that way," I said again. Then, cupping my hands, I called out, "Meg! Where are you?"

"We better look for this young girl before we worry about the thief," said the officer. "Call for backup," he said to the other officer. Then he turned to us and said, "You kids come with me."

Handing a flashlight to me and grabbing another for himself, the officer ran toward the woods. Marion turned back toward the hotel lobby and said, "I'll call your folks," but the three of us kids were right behind the officer.

"Her name is Meg?" he asked.

"That's right," said Shauna.

As soon as we got to the edge of the parking lot the officer began shining his light into the thick stand of trees. We all began calling her name again as loudly as we could. Walking in a wide line next to each other we entered the woods. The police officer was on one end of our line and I was on the other. He was sweeping the light back and forth in large slow movements in front of us as we moved forward. I copied the motion with the flashlight that he had given to me.

The thing that had always amazed me about this part of the United States was the thick forests of trees everywhere. I forget that we live in a barren desert until we come to places like this. In Utah, there are lots of wide open areas that are usually just covered with wild grass and sagebrush. But in the East it seemed like anyplace there wasn't a building or a road, there were trees. And not just a few trees, either—there were lots and lots of big, tall trees.

We must have been searching and calling out to Meg for at least twenty minutes when the officer who was with us got a call on his radio.

"Your parents are here," the officer said. "Let's go back to the hotel."

While we were looking for Meg, Marion had phoned Rudy and Chloe to tell them what was going on. I guess Mom and Dad had just gotten to their house, so Marion gave them directions to the hotel. When we got back to the parking lot there were at least six or seven police cars, all with their emergency lights flashing. The officers were organizing themselves into search teams and heading out into the woods. Shauna, Brandon, and I didn't get to go with them this time, though. There were other officers there who wanted to hear everything that had happened from the time that Anthony first came into Chloe and Rudy's house.

We all went inside the hotel lobby and answered all of their questions as they filled out their police reports. Mom and Dad just sat quietly with open mouths and wide eyes as we told the police the story. I think they were pretty amazed by the whole thing. But I noticed Mom kept glancing out into the parking lot. I think more than anything, she was worried about Meg. I had to agree.

We showed them Anthony's car, and the police started to search it. We told them about the document that had started this whole thing, and they found it almost immediately. It looked like the copy that we had seen on the seat of this car when we first found it in the parking lot of our hotel in New York. The police also found the letter that had been stolen from our hotel room in Canada.

"Sounds like it's time to call in the FBI," said one of the officers.

While Dad explained to the officers why the FBI already knew about all this, Brandon and I went with two other officers and the hotel manager up to Anthony's room where we explained everything that happened while we were there. The officers told Brandon and me to head back downstairs while they started searching the room.

Back in the parking lot we found Dad talking to one of the police officers. When Dad was finished, he said, "Climb in the van for a few minutes, guys. We're going to have a family prayer."

When we got inside the van, we found that everyone else was already there—everyone except for Meg, of course. It's amazing how empty the van felt, having just one fewer than we were used to.

"We're going to have a prayer for Meg," Dad explained after he closed the door behind him. Dad said the prayer. He pleaded with Heavenly Father to protect Meg from Dr. Anthony and to bring her safely back to us. He prayed especially hard that Meg would be comforted and not feel afraid and that she would be guided to know where to go and what to do.

When the prayer ended, Mom said, "It's important to remember that Meg is a very smart girl. She makes good decisions."

"That's right," Shauna agreed. "She knows how to take care of herself."

"She's amazing," I said. "I can't believe all the stuff she knows."

We spent the next few minutes talking about Meg and everything that was wonderful about her. Then we each took a turn saying a prayer out loud for her. I'm always surprised by the peace that I feel whenever I pray about something that's really important. It just gives me the impression that no matter how things turn out, God is watching over us and will do whatever is best for us.

When we were done talking and praying, Dad agreed to stay in the van with Danny and Chelsea. They were tired and were starting to fall asleep. The rest of us went out to join the search for Meg. We decided to all stay together as we searched. The police gave us a flashlight and a map and sent us to a certain place to begin looking. He told us to check back in an hour. Meg had already been missing for at least an hour by this time.

As we walked together, shining our flashlight everywhere we could and calling out Meg's name, I started to think about everything that had happened. The peaceful feeling that had been there when we prayed was gone now, and I was starting to feel really bad about what had happened.

"I guess I shouldn't have thrown that thing down to her," I said to Mom.

"No," Mom said. "There's no point in talking about what things could have been different or what things we should or shouldn't have done."

I just nodded in silence, even though I knew she wouldn't be able to see me in the dark.

"You did what came to you in the moment," Mom said. "It's important to follow the feelings and ideas that come to us. Meg is lost right now—and that's a terrible thing—but no one can say what might have happened if you hadn't thrown that pouch to her."

I didn't say anything. Neither did anyone else.

"You and Brandon were stuck in a room with a criminal," Mom said. "He's been in prison. He had a gun. And obviously he hasn't changed his attitude about breaking the law. You two could have easily been killed or seriously hurt up there. Meg may have just saved your lives."

"I hadn't thought of it that way," I mumbled. That almost made me feel even worse.

"We'll find her," Mom said. "We'll find her before the night is through. I know it."

Mom stopped for a moment and shined the flashlight on the map the police officer had given us. "Where do you think we are?" she asked.

Shauna pointed and said, "I think we're right about here."

"Is that the Interstate?" Mom asked, pointing to a double line going along the edge of the map.

"It looks like it," Shauna said. "Oh, yeah, it is. It says 'I-90' right there."

"If she was close to the Interstate," Mom said, "then she wouldn't be able to hear us calling to her very well."

"Do you think we should look over there?" I asked.

Mom was quiet for a moment and then said, "Yes. Let's go."

We headed toward the Interstate and continued calling Meg's name every few seconds. The sounds of the passing cars became louder and louder. There were lights along this part of the Interstate, and we were able to pick our way quite easily. We walked along the edge of the trees for quite a while when suddenly I thought I heard something.

"Stop, everyone!" I said, holding out my arms to the sides. They all froze in place. Then I heard it again.

"Mom!" came Meg's voice faintly.

"Meg!" Mom called. "We're here! Where are you?"

"Over here!" came the soft answer from somewhere in the trees.

We all ran as quickly as we dared in the direction of the sound of her voice. It was dark among the trees, and the underbrush was so thick we weren't able to move very fast at all. Within a minute or so we found Meg lying on the ground, halfway leaning up against a tree. She was shivering terribly.

"Are you okay?" Mom asked her.

"I hurt my head," Meg said quietly. She sounded exhausted and like she was in a lot of pain.

Mom shined the flashlight on her and we were shocked to see both dried and wet blood on her forehead and running down the side of her face.

"What happened?" Mom breathed softly.

"I slipped on a wet rock in a little stream," Meg explained between shivers. "I fell in and hit my head and got all wet."

Mom reached around her and picked her up.

"You're soaked," Mom said.

"I'm cold," Meg said.

"Did you see Dr. Anthony?" Shauna asked.

"Uh-huh," Meg said softly.

"Did he hurt you?" Mom asked.

"Nuh-uh," Meg mumbled. "He never saw me." She drew a deep breath, then she said, "I saw him climb the fence and go to the freeway and get a ride."

"Alright," Mom said. "Let's get back to where we can clean you up, okay?"

"Okay," Meg said, snuggling in. She sounded like she was falling asleep.

"Can I carry your backpack for you?" I asked.

Without speaking, Meg wriggled around in Mom's arms, pulling her backpack from her shoulders. She handed it to me, and we all started walking back toward the hotel.

After about thirty seconds, Meg said quietly, "The pouch isn't in there, though. I hid it by the root of Lehi's tree."

"Don't talk," Mom whispered to her. "We can worry about all that later."

It took probably close to fifteen minutes to get back to the hotel. We each took turns carrying Meg. She never said another word, but fell asleep in Mom's arms and didn't wake up even when she was moved from one person to another.

After wrapping Meg up in a blanket, the police put Mom and Meg in the back of one of their cars and drove them to the hospital. One of them looked carefully at Meg's head and said that she was going to need stitches, but that the wound wasn't really too bad. Shauna and Brandon and I climbed inside the van with Dad and followed the police car.

"Where are Chelsea and Danny?" I asked.

"I just barely got back from taking them to Chloe and Rudy's house," Dad said. "They're spending the night in their extra bedroom. I was about to come join the search. But this is even better. Now we can all go to the hospital together and see how Meg is doing."

We followed Mom and Meg into the emergency waiting room. I've never seen anyone shiver in their sleep before, but that's what Meg was doing. She didn't even wake up when the doctor stitched up her head. Because she had been hit on the head and was sleeping, the doctor said he wanted to keep her overnight for observation. Mom stayed with Meg while Dad took the rest of us to our hotel room.

Apparently Mom and Dad had checked into the hotel before they came to Chloe and Rudy's. That was nice, because that meant we could all just go right in and drop into bed without having to wait for anything. It was almost 4:00 A.M. before we finally got there. They had checked back into the same hotel where we stayed when we first got to Cleveland the week before. I was pleased to learn that we had another two-bedroom suite. I don't know how anyone else felt, but I was exhausted and fell asleep within about three and a half seconds of lying down.

A few hours later, I woke up with a start. It was kind of like when you have a dream that you're falling somewhere and you jerk so bad that you wake yourself up. But I didn't dream that I was falling—I dreamt that Anthony was back in the woods looking for the pouch. I looked over at the clock. It read 8:53 A.M.

I had been sleeping on the sofa bed in the family room. Dad was sitting at the kitchen table investigating something in his blue binder.

"Good morning, Jeff," he smiled. "How are you feeling?"

"Nervous," I said.

Dad just stared at me as he blinked several times. "About what?" he finally asked.

"I'll tell you in a minute," I said, rubbing my face in an attempt to get the sand goobies out of the corners of my eyes. "But first, do you know how Meg is?"

"I talked to Mom just a few minutes ago," Dad said. "The doctors think she will be fine, but they're not ready to release her from the hospital yet."

"That's great about Meg," I said, heaving a sigh. I was relieved to hear the news. But now something else was bothering me. "Can we go back to the woods and look for the pouch?"

"I'm glad you asked that," Dad said. "The police are there, now. They called a few minutes ago and asked if we would come help them look for it. They're anxious to find it for evidence."

"Did they talk to Meg?" I asked.

"Get showered," Dad said. "I'll tell you the whole story on the way."

It turned out that Brandon was just getting out of the shower. Dad was going to wait until he was out before waking me up, so I woke up just at the right time. Shauna was in the other shower.

"So what's going on?" Shauna asked as we all climbed into the van.

Shauna was in the front seat across from Dad, while Brandon and I were on the front bench, leaning forward to hear what Dad was saying.

"The police are anxious to get the pouch back for two reasons," Dad said. "One is the fact that no one knows what's in it and what its value is. The other is because they need it as evidence in the charges against Mr. Anthony."

"Did they catch him?" I asked hopefully.

"Not yet," said Dad.

"Have they talked to Meg?" Shauna asked.

"I guess they tried," Dad said, "but the doctor is being very protective of her right now. She was awake earlier but apparently she seemed pretty disoriented and confused. The doctor wants to let her sleep some more and then see if she seems better."

"But the police don't want to wait?" Shauna asked.

"They're very uptight about Mr. Anthony," Dad explained. "They just want to find the pouch as soon as they can. Mom said she remembered Meg saying something about hiding the pouch at the root of a tree."

"Meg said that she hid the pouch by the root of *Lehi's* tree," Shauna said.

"Lehi?" Dad asked. He nodded for a moment and said, "The police officer who called said that they have found quite a few trees with various names and other strange words on them that look like they were painted on with silver nail polish. Does Meg carry silver nail polish in her backpack?"

"She carries *everything* in her backpack," Brandon said.

"I'm pretty sure she had some in there," Shauna agreed.

"Was 'Lehi' one of the names?" I asked. "Did he tell you what the names were?"

"He said a couple like 'Joseph,' and 'Adam,' and something else," Dad said. "But to him 'Lehi' would probably have been one of the strange words; I doubt he would have recognized it as a name."

"I'll bet she wrote the name *Lehi* on a tree," Shauna said.

We talked about it the rest of the way to Anthony's hotel.

There were still four or five police cars in the parking lot when we arrived.

"Looks like you weren't kidding about them being anxious," I said.

"Well, I'm sure they want to find it before anyone else does," Dad nodded as he turned off the van and climbed out.

We were met by a police officer who had been coordinating everything that they had found on the trees so far. The other officers were radioing to him each word they found along with the location of the tree that had the word on it. Apparently, Meg had been very busy. He showed us a list of all the words they had found so far. They were *Joseph, Lehi, Nephi, Mosiah, Adam, Moroni, Mormon, Zoram, Helaman, Alma,* and *Sam.*

"They also found a tree that had what looked like a scripture reference on it and another tree that had a drawing of a tree on it," the officer said.

"Really?" said Dad. "Was there anything around the drawing of the tree?"

"Yeah," said the officer. "There was what looked like a river and a path and stick figures of people standing by the tree."

Shauna started to laugh. "That's Lehi's tree of life."

"Oh, yeah!" I said.

"So do you think that's where the missing pouch is?" asked the officer. "My people have been searching around the roots of every tree they find with these words and drawings on them."

"Well," said Shauna. "She told us last night that she hid it by the root of Lehi's tree."

The officer quickly scanned the list of words and pointed to the word *Lehi.*

"Is that how you pronounce this word?" he asked.

"Yes," Dad said.

Excited, the officer pressed the button on the microphone hooked to his shoulder and said, "I think we've got something here.

Try the tree with the word L-E-H-I on it." He spelled the word, rather than trying to pronounce it. The officer smiled at us as he released the button on the microphone.

"Thanks for your help folks," he said. We waited for a few moments and then heard the response come back through his radio.

"There's nothing here," came a female voice. "Are you sure?"

"Wait a minute," I said. "What have we been talking about this whole trip?"

Everyone just stared at me for a minute.

"Family history?" Shauna finally asked.

"Exactly!" I smiled.

Shauna just stared at me for a moment and then, with a look of sudden understanding on her face, she said, "Oh! Family trees!" She paused with excitement, her eyes darting about. "The root of Lehi's *family* tree!"

"Right!" I nodded. "And when Lehi got the plates of Laban, he found out that he was a descendant of Joseph!"

The officer quickly scanned the list and then said into the microphone, "Look at the root of the tree with the name 'Joseph' on it." When he looked back at us he said, "Looks like we have it now."

"But wait," Brandon scowled. "Didn't Mom say that Elias Franzen was the root of our family tree because that was as far back as we could trace him?"

"We haven't found any trees with the name 'Elias Franzen' on them," said the officer, consulting his notepad.

"I know," said Brandon impatiently. "What I'm saying is that Joseph was not as far back as Lehi could trace his family tree."

"Oh, you're right!" said Shauna. "Once he knew that he was a descendant of Joseph, then he would be able to trace his line all the way back to Adam!" Looking hesitantly over at Dad, she asked, "Wouldn't he?"

206

Dad smiled and nodded. Just then another voice came over the officer's radio.

"We're not finding anything near the roots of the 'Joseph' tree, either," came the voice.

"I know," said the officer in his microphone. "We just figured that out. Try 'Adam.'"

"Are you serious?" came the response. "At this rate, we might as well be checking them all—which is what we've been doing anyway."

"Just do it!" replied the officer. I looked down to see if he was wearing Nike tennis shoes. He wasn't.

"Wait," said Dad. "*Adam* is the root of Lehi's tree. Tell them not to look at the root of the tree, but tell them to look somewhere near the name itself."

The officer looked a little reluctant, but finally he said into the microphone, "Don't look at the roots of the tree. Look up higher."

We all waited for what seemed like at least a full minute. Then a woman's voice came over the radio, saying, "I think we've got it! Is it a brown leather pouch about the size of a man's wallet when it's laid open?"

"That's it!" I said. Shauna and Brandon both said it with me at the same time.

"I think that's it," said the officer into his microphone. "Bring it in!"

CHAPTER 17

The Forgotten Treasure

We waited anxiously for about five minutes until the officer returned with the pouch.

"That's it!" Brandon said with excitement as the officer approached.

"Where was it?" Dad asked.

"It was about eight feet up in the tree," said the officer. "She must have thrown it up there. I don't think anyone would have ever found it if she hadn't marked the tree." As the police officer handed the pouch to the officer in charge, she said, "Shall we have a look inside it, since the owners are here?"

"We're not the owners," Dad said. "This belongs to the people who live in the house where it was found."

"Are you speaking of Rudy and Chloe?" asked the officer.

Dad nodded.

"I left their home about an hour ago," one of the officers said to Dad. "They were on their way to the hospital to visit your daughter. I guess they have your two youngest children with them already."

"Well, let's go then," smiled Dad. "We haven't seen any of them yet today."

The officer placed the pouch inside a large manila envelope and sealed it shut. Then we all climbed into the van and followed the police car to the hospital. I was sort of hoping he would use his lights and siren to get us there quicker, but he didn't. I had started to think about Meg again, and I was worried about what Dad had said earlier. Maybe her injury was worse than anyone had originally thought.

When we got to Meg's hospital room we found a party. Marion was there, as was Chloe, Chelsea, Danny, and Mom. Meg was wide awake and seemed perfectly fine. She let us all look at the stitches that she had on top of her head, just above her hairline.

After Meg had assured everyone that she felt great, Dad said, "Thanks for the little puzzle out in the woods."

Meg smiled. "Did you find the pouch?" she asked anxiously.

"It's right inside this envelope," said the police officer.

Meg heaved a huge sigh of relief and breathed, "Oh, good!"

The officer handed the envelope to Chloe and said, "I'm told this is yours. Where's your husband?"

Chloe smiled and said, "He went downstairs to get me some grape juice. He'll be back in a few minutes."

Then the officer asked, "Do you think you might look inside it now? I'm sure we're all anxious to see exactly what all this fuss has been about."

"I reckon we should wait for Rudy," said Chloe. "He's the one who's going to have to fix the hole in the wall. He ought to be here when we all find out what he found in there."

"Meg," Brandon said, "I just want to know one thing: why did you hide the pouch and then write things all over the trees?"

Meg smiled. "I was afraid that Dr. Anthony would find me and take the pouch away. So I climbed a tree and hid the pouch on one of the limbs. But it was so dark I was afraid I wouldn't be able to remember which tree it was. After I climbed back down I decided I just better mark the tree so that we could find it when it was light."

"No wonder the police couldn't find it," I said. "They kept looking around the roots of all the trees."

"I used my silver nail polish," Meg explained, "because it was the one I could see the best with my tiny flashlight."

"I was wondering about that!" I said.

"Did you like my clue?" Meg asked with sparkling eyes.

"It was great!" Dad said, but it took us a while to figure it out. "How did you think of it?"

"When Mom told us that Elias Franzen was the root of our family tree," Meg explained. "I started thinking about how great it will be when we know *all* of our forefathers all the way back to Adam and then *he* will be the root of our family tree." Meg smiled. "Then right after that, we started talking about Lehi knowing his genealogy, and it just made me think that Adam was the root of Lehi's family tree." She smiled again and then shrugged. "But I don't know why I thought about that when I was out there in the woods. I just did."

"Were you afraid?" Dad asked.

"No," Meg said. "Because I prayed. And because I heard the man again."

We all waited for her to continue.

"Do you remember the man who told me not to tell the FBI men about the message I wrote down? That same man told me that I would be safe and that Mr. Anthony wouldn't find me."

"I'm glad you weren't scared," Mom smiled at Meg.

"Me, too," said Meg. "And then I started wondering which one of our forefathers he was. Maybe that's why I thought to put the words on the trees."

"But why did you put so many different names all over so many trees?" Brandon asked.

"In case Mr. Anthony came looking," Meg said with a somber face. "If only one tree had something on it, then he would know where to look."

Just then a young man we didn't know came to the door of Meg's room and said, "Excuse me. Are you the Andrews family?"

He looked a lot like a returned missionary who hadn't been home very long.

"Yes," Dad answered. "How can we help you?"

"I just came to apologize," he said. "I think all this trouble that you've had here is my fault. I'm Paul Mauer. I'm the one who gave Dr. Anthony a copy of the document from the archive."

"Oh, I see," nodded Dad.

"The FBI tracked me down on my vacation," the young man said. "I'm sure they haven't told me everything that's been going on—but what I know is already bad enough. I really want to apologize."

"It's not your fault," Dad said. "You don't need to apologize for anything. You're fine."

"You came all the way from Utah just to apologize?" asked Mom. "How thoughtful. Don't you agree, Shauna?"

Shauna didn't say anything, so I looked over at her. She had a really strange look on her face. She was staring right at the guy with her mouth hanging slightly open. She didn't blink.

"I was actually already in the area," said Paul. "I see so many Church historical documents in my job and have Church history on my mind so much that I come out here almost every summer."

"So you work for the Church archive department?" Mom asked.

"Just part time," said Paul. "I've been there for a couple of years—ever since I got home from my mission. I'm actually a full-time history major at the University of Utah."

"Oh," smiled Mom, pointing toward Shauna. "Our daughter just finished her freshman year at BYU."

"Really?" said Paul. "What's your major?"

"Computer science," said Shauna, finally able to speak. She seemed a little embarrassed.

"Cool!" said Paul. "If I come down to visit you after we all get back to Utah, will you give me a tour of the BYU campus?"

"Sure!" smiled Shauna.

Then Paul asked, "Does it bother you that I'm a history major?"

"No way," said Shauna. "All the CS majors I know are geeks."

"Oh," said Paul, "I know people like that. They're the ones who take a laptop computer with them on vacations, right? Do you do that?"

"Well," said Shauna, "I brought one—but it's mostly to watch movies on." She paused, looking even more embarrassed. Then she said, "But it's not even mine. I borrowed it from . . . someone." Then her face brightened as she said, "In fact, when you come for that tour of BYU, you can come with me to give it back, if you want."

It was then that I realized what that funny look on Shauna's face was for! I started to say something to Brandon about what I thought was going on inside Shauna's head, but just then Rudy walked in.

"We've been waiting for you," said Chloe, handing Rudy the manila envelope with the pouch inside.

"Ah!" smiled Rudy at the police officer. "You found it!"

"It's quite a story," said Chloe. "I'll tell you when we get home. But right now we all want to see what is inside there."

Rudy tore open the manila envelope and carefully removed the leather pouch. This was the first time any of us had gotten a good look at it. It was stitched all the way around the outer edges with a strip of thin leather. The outer flap was held in place with two leather straps that were wrapped around the entire pouch and tied together in a square knot.

Rudy carefully untied the knot and laid the flap back. Reaching inside he pulled out a stack of colored paper that looked to me like play money. It wasn't like anything I'd ever seen before.

Marion looked closely at it and said, "It looks like it might be the real thing."

"Really?" said Rudy. Carefully leafing through the stack of notes, Rudy added, "They all have 'Bank of the United States' printed on them. It looks like most are from the Philadelphia branch, but some are from New Orleans."

"I know a dealer in Cleveland," said Marion. "We can take it to him and find out what it's all worth."

"Hey, what's that?" I asked, pointing to the pouch. Inside the open flap were several words burned lightly into the leather.

Rudy picked up the pouch and read the words aloud to us. Inside the pouch was written:

Fashioned by the hand of Graham Thomas Franzen for my son, Elias.

There was dead silence in the room for at least two full seconds. Then Mom said with excitement, "Do you realize what we just found?"

"What?" asked Chelsea.

"The name of Elias Franzen's dad!" Mom beamed.

Chelsea drew a huge breath and said with wide eyes, "We found his daddy?"

"Elias isn't the root of our tree anymore," said Meg.

We talked about it for a couple of minutes, excited by the possibilities. When there seemed to be a break in the conversation, Rudy said to Mom, "We'll get an appraisal of the value of this money and let you know as soon as possible."

Mom just shook her head as she said, "The money is yours. The name of Graham Thomas Franzen is the only treasure we've been looking for."

"Well," said the police officer, "I guess if there's nothing else, I'll be leaving now. Thanks to each of you for your help."

"I have a question," I said to the officer. He stopped in the doorway and looked over at me. "What was the scripture reference you said one of the officers found?"

He reached into his shirt pocket, pulled out his notepad, and flipped through the pages.

"It looks like Jacob 2:18–19," he said. He looked up from the paper and said, "I don't remember a book of Jacob in the Bible."

"Probably not," smiled Dad. "Thanks for your time."

The officer gave a little salute and left.

"What was that scripture for?" Dad asked Meg.

"It was for Mr. Anthony," Meg said.

"What does it say?" I asked.

Meg just shrugged. "Something," she finally said. Obviously we were going to have to find it for ourselves.

"Where's your backpack, Meg?" Brandon asked, looking around the room and pulling open the small closet. "You have your little scriptures in there, right?"

"I think it's still in the van," Dad smiled.

Brandon grunted his disappointment. Looking again at Meg, he asked, "Are you going to tell us what it says?"

Meg pretended to yawn and then said, "The doctor told me to get some rest."

"Dad," I asked, "may I borrow the keys to the van?"

Pulling the keys from his pocket and tossing them to me, Dad said, "Don't take it anywhere."

Ignoring his comment, I thanked him for the keys, and Brandon and I raced down the hall toward the van.

About the Author

Carl Blaine Andersen holds a bachelor of science degree and a master's degree in mechanical engineering from Brigham Young University and is a software engineer at Novell. A former member of the Mormon Youth Symphony, Carl enjoys music and teaches cello. He has served in The Church of Jesus Christ of Latter-day Saints in various ward and stake callings and as a full-time missionary in the Switzerland Zurich Mission. He is married to Shari Lynn Tillery Andersen. They are the parents of six children and reside in Orem, Utah. Brother Andersen maintains an Internet Web site dedicated to these books and welcomes your comments and questions: www.cbandersen.net